CARDS OF LOVE: JUSTICE

CARDS OF LOVE: JUSTICE

AMELIA WILDE

Cover Design: Lori Jackson Design

Editing: Write Way Creative

Proofreading: Cassie Hess-Dean

Promotional Graphics: Tempting Illustrations

For Justice and Cassian, who wouldn't let me quit.

1

*T*his is the night I make my escape.

The silver balloon shoots up from the net like a diver swimming the hell away from an undiscovered deep-sea animal—too fast, way too fast, fast enough to get the bends—and hurls itself against the steel rafters, exploding like a shot.

At least, I assume it sounds like a gunshot. I can't hear anything over the deafening roar of the music at this party. It's so loud that it thrums through my ears and into my jaw, rattling my teeth.

It's time to go.

For one thing, I'm crashing this party.

For another, the balloon release is the signal.

The birthday girl, according to the signs in the lobby, was born at exactly 12:05 a.m. Perfect timing.

I have no idea why she wanted to ring in her freshly minted adulthood at *this* second-rate club—with a balloon release, no less—but her friends are still screaming their congratulations when I unfold myself from the booth, gather my purse, and begin wending my way to the doors.

Justice Danes is *out*.

Out of this party.

Out of Manhattan.

And out of all the awful things I've done.

All the awful things my family has made me do.

But did they really *make* me, or—

Now's not the time for debate—not if I want to follow through with this plan and flee the city for somewhere better. Somewhere that doesn't make my skin feel stained from the past.

My heart picks up the pace the closer I get to the narrow cast-iron stairs leading down to the main floor. The plan itself makes nominal sense, in that I know my personal security guard, Andre, loathes this kind of party. An hour ago, I pouted at him until he agreed to wait in the car.

I'm never going back to that car.

The first floor of the club is a sea of people who should be too young to get into a bar, much less be this drunk. I wouldn't mind a buzz at this point, but I have been fucking steadfast. Not even a sip of a vodka cranberry has graced my lips this evening. I left the entire thing sitting on the table as a kind of sacrifice to the gods of getting the fuck out of here.

In the hallway leading to the bathrooms—and beyond that, the kitchen—a clutch of drunk high school seniors descends upon me.

"Oh, my *God*," one of them trills. "Chelsea." My name is not Chelsea. "I fucking love you. You used to be so fucking ugly. Get in the picture." She flops her arm around my neck and presses her slobbery lips to my cheek. Somewhere in front of us, a camera flashes. There's a 50-50 chance it captures my blank, horrified expression.

"I love you, too," I tell her, digging my fingers into her arm and twisting it off of me.

"Like, *ow*," she says, narrowing her eyes to glower at me. Then her face lights up. "Are you going to get drinks?"

"Yeah." I paste on my biggest, brightest smile. "What do you want?"

She tips her head back like she's in the throes of a halfway decent orgasm, her hair all ruffled on one side from dancing. "Like...anything with Red Bull."

"Got it. I'll be right back."

"Love you, Chels," she calls after me.

I will not be right back.

For appearance sake, I pause outside the bathroom and pretend to look inside my clutch. The posse of drunken teens is gone when I look up, so I don't have to waste any more time. I head past the bathrooms, take a hard left, and stride with confidence toward the swinging kitchen door.

It's a sturdier door than I thought, because when I push it open and step over the threshold, the volume of the music drops. Or maybe it's just so quiet in here that it sucks up all the sound and folds it into the silence.

A door creaks open to my left.

"Hey!"

"I'm on my way out," I tell whoever it is.

"You're not allowed to be back here."

"I don't want to be back here." I risk a glance. You can never be too careful when you're making an escape. It's a lanky guy with a dark shirt and an apron, and he's balancing a stack of metal bowls in his arms.

"They're always drunk," he mumbles, and I push open the back door and step out into the alley.

My first inhale of the night air smells more like a rancid garbage dump than freedom. It's disgusting back here.

Not that I needed another reason to walk out onto the sidewalk.

It's the part of the block nobody's supposed to see. Paper tumbleweeds grown from shredded posters blow up to the foot of the one street light. The bulb is blown out, so I have to navigate my way under the light pollution that hangs over Manhattan.

Soon, I'll be...elsewhere.

Destination so far unknown, but a few of the details are nonnegotiable. Clean air. Sheets of an appropriate thread count. And an address my family knows nothing about. Where my father and brother can never find me again. For all I know, my brother Hector is already in charge, has already stepped up to take my dad's place. Maybe they celebrated the promotion tonight. Either way, I want to be gone by the time they realize they need me again.

Maybe I'll finally have a chance to find my sister.

But I have to push Patience out of my head along with everyone else. Tonight isn't about them. It's about me.

I have enough money tucked into my purse to make it to where Tripp is waiting, and then some. Once I had a nanny who drilled it into me that I should always carry some cash. In case of what, I didn't know. Why would I need money when Andre was everywhere I went?

The fall breeze swirls around the points of my heels, and I hurry faster.

Three blocks—that's all it is.

A car goes by one block behind, and I tuck my head down and walk faster. I look like an idiot out here without a coat, but I couldn't carry one inside the club without tipping off Andre. I could have stolen one, I guess, but then one of those wasted 18-year-olds would be freezing her ass off out here.

I might be the black sheep of my family, but I try my best not to be a bitch. Enjoy your coat, drunk girl.

I wait for the traffic signal—which, why?—and go quickly across the crosswalk.

That's when I feel them.

The eyes.

Someone's watching me.

No. Nobody's watching me. It's late, it's cold, it's October —nobody *cares* what's going on at midnight. Nobody knows I'm here, anyway. Nobody knows what my plan is or where I'm going with Tripp. Nobody knows how done I am with this life, with my father, with all of their bullshit.

Nobody knows how done I am waiting for the shoe to drop.

"They don't know," I repeat to myself out loud, the words swept away from my lips by the wind. "Nobody knows."

Nobody knows, except Tripp.

There's no realistic reason to think that anybody's watching or following me. That's fucking paranoid.

Those are not footsteps that I hear.

Other than mine, those are not—

I stop abruptly in the middle of the sidewalk, and two heavy footfalls echo off the brick buildings to my left.

My heart rockets up into my throat. It's two more blocks. Fine—two and a half. I can run if I have to, but I'm not going to run. Running only makes people take chase. But I move faster—as fast as I can without breaking into a jog. My ankles ache from the sheer height of my shoes.

Two blocks.

I throw myself out into the street without waiting for the light, and someone behind me breathes audibly.

It's one inhale, the sound of someone who maybe doesn't believe I can walk this fast in heels, and a fresh wave of goose bumps rises at the back of my neck.

Coincidence.

Somebody else is out here, looking for a cab. Hurrying home. Probably escaping that party, too. No reason to think—

They break into a run.

I know it from the first scrape of their shoe on the sidewalk, know it from the way I've got one and a half blocks to the car.

Run. Run. *Run.*

Half a block to go. The short, sequined dress that was supposed to be *so* perfect to blend in at the club rides up to the bottom of my ass, letting the cold air sweep between my legs. It freezes me to the core.

My right heel catches.

It just...catches in the crack of the sidewalk. I scramble to get upright, scramble to keep my balance, but my ankle twists and I go down hard to the left. Pain scrapes up my left elbow and *Jesus,* that hurts as much as it did when I was a kid. I shove off and up, breath ragged, and this is it —this is the final sprint, everything I've got, half a block, half a fucking *block*—

I reach the corner.

The entire intersection is soaked with the yellow glow of a flickering street lamp.

The entire intersection is empty.

There's no car here, no one is here waiting for me.

Why. *Why?*

I don't have time to figure out the answer.

I lurch forward, ready to run across the street, ready to try one more time, and that's when the hand closes over my mouth—gloved. Andre never wears gloves. It's not my bodyguard. I take one heaving breath through my nose and I'm met with silence, not Andre's exasperated scolding.

That's when I know I have been caught.

2

CASSIAN

*M*y shoulder hurts.

It's a burn that reminds me of lifting the final set of weights in the gym, but it's concentrated in my right arm. I'll have to do something about that imbalance, and it vaguely irritates me that I can't reproduce it exactly.

Not that my last contract would have been able to withstand that.

I can still hear her crying.

It was a one-week session and she cried every time. I was tired of the tears by Wednesday, but the payers certainly weren't. They got their money's worth.

I key in the code on the door to the rest of my apartment and push the door open with the flat of my palm. She can cry in the stairwell—a private exit and entrance off a secluded alleyway—for another five minutes, if she likes. I don't need to hear it. I'll send the security team to remove her if she doesn't leave.

They always leave.

Some take longer than others.

This one, at least, had someone to collect her other than a driver idling in the alleyway. It's David's job to take their trembling bodies from the paddling bench and take them to the person on the landing at the top of the stairs or to the concrete step that marks the last boundary of this house.

I should do something about my underused left arm, but I'm fucking tired. My job is far more complicated than David's. Mine is to bend and punish and break the people —mostly women—who are sent to me. My job is to remain impassive. Remaining impassive is the easiest and the hardest part.

I should go down to the gym. I don't.

It's been a long week, and the burn in my shoulder curves its way around the back of my neck and down my spine. It's time to shut the door of my suite and lock it behind me—past time. The last session ran long. I was paid a handsome bonus. It's enough for tonight. More than enough.

The hallway opens up into the main living room, the one with the elevator into the main lobby. Firelight pours from the fireplace. It bathes the room in enough flickering, orange light for me to know that Lysander isn't here.

Thank God.

I'm not interested in conversation with my brother at this moment.

I move down the hall, lifting one hand to rub at my shoulder. The double doors leading to the bedroom suites are firmly closed. If I can just make it to those doors, no one will bother me.

The universe, in all of its infinite power and wisdom, favors me up until the moment I reach for the door handle.

The door swings open unbidden.

And there he is on the other side—the very brother I'd hoped to avoid.

"Good night," I tell him, crisply, tersely, hoping it's enough to get him to move out of my way.

It's not.

"Cash." He puts one hand up on the doorframe as if that could ever stop me from going where I want. "Is the last contract out?"

"Of course she's out. I finished with her half an hour ago."

"Good. Good." He rubs his hands together, eyes bright. "Has Lily been in yet?"

I look at him through narrowed eyes. "It's been thirty minutes," I say levelly. This is not entirely true. I don't care. "It's after midnight. It can wait until morning."

"It can't."

The fatigue gathering behind my eyes crystallizes and disappears. "What the hell are you talking about?"

Lysander, I'm seeing now, looks too proud of himself for this to be mere satisfaction at a job well done. "We have someone coming in. Right now."

"No, we don't. I haven't signed any new contracts." I was going to leave the city for a week or two, but I haven't mentioned that to Lysander yet. I don't intend to take him with me. It's enough to be living in the same apartment with him. It's enough to be in business with him. I'll admit that he does have some specific skills that balance mine out, but I find his entrepreneurial spirit exhausting.

I have never needed an entrepreneurial spirit. When I took over this business for my father, I did so with the knowledge that New York City's elites will never want for drama and intrigue. They'll forever have their claws at each other's throats. And I'll be here, waiting to dispense the only kind of justice they can tolerate.

The kind that happens behind closed doors. In private rooms. For a price high enough to make me the impartial arbiter.

No—that's not quite true, either. They negotiate among themselves. They agree on the length of punishments, of severity. The fine details are always left up to me. As they should be. I'm the one who carries them out.

"I did."

"You did what?"

"I signed a new contract."

I make it a point in my life not to entertain emotional reactions, but what the fuck? "When?"

"While you were in with...her."

We usually call those people deposited on the landing, arms crossed tightly in front of their chests, *the contracts.* It's not an elegant term. It's not meant to be. It's meant to be passionless. And it is.

I shove down my irritation to the far reaches of my mind and resist the urge to ask Lysander why he's signing contracts if he can't follow protocol. "While I was with the contract, you sat down with two parties, entertained negotiations, and—"

"I signed a contract," Lysander insists. "And she's coming now."

"I never agree to contracts on such short notice."

"There was a bonus."

The way he smiles when he says it tells me that it was substantial. It also sets off a warning bell in the back of my mind—an obnoxious peal that makes the muscles up and down my back tighten. "This isn't wise."

"It's already done." Lysander sticks his hands in his pockets. He's fully dressed, so either he's planned to go out, or he's planned to do...something else. "If you're not up to the task, I'm more than willing to—"

"No."

He frowns. "You know, Cash, you're not going to be able to control this forever. At some point, you'll need to let me step in and—"

"No. The moment you walk into that room is the moment all of this crumbles around us."

"Jesus Christ." Anger flares on his face, red spots splotch his cheeks. "Do you always have to be such an asshole? I brought in enough money to cover—"

"We're past that," I tell him through gritted teeth. "When are you going to wake up? We're past *hustling* for other jobs to make ends meet. What did you expect me to do? Pat you on the head and hand over the reins? You're fucking dreaming, Lys."

He blows a short breath out through his nose. "It's not my fault if I don't want to follow in our dad's footsteps."

I want to punch him. The bright, sharp feeling scrapes its edge along my shoulder blades. It's all I can do to hold it at arm's length, letting it cut into my palms instead. "At least he understood the importance of maintaining our professional distance. That means not taking on contracts like a desperate beggar."

Lysander changes tactics again. "I can deal with it," he says humbly. "You were on your way to your room. I'm more than capable of setting things up so that—"

"That's not how we do things." I stare into his eyes, daring him to argue with me.

For a long moment, he holds my gaze, his matching dark eyes hard on mine.

But it doesn't last.

It never does.

His eyes slide to the floor, and then to his watch. "She'll be here any second. Justice Danes."

"Then I have work to do." I turn on my heel, the sound of the name ringing like a bell in my mind. The moment my reckless, irresponsible brother's face is out of my sight a weight lifts, like it was a yoke around my neck. "We'll discuss this in the morning."

"It's a done deal," he says to my back. "You know that."

I fucking do know that, but I'm not going to give him the satisfaction.

Back through the living room I go. Lysander doesn't follow me.

The door into the contract wing is coded from both sides, and I punch the numbers in while I swallow the bitter dregs of my own frustration. I hate that sensation—that loss of control. But I've practiced long enough that I can paint it over in my mind in a matter of seconds.

Through the door and into the hallway. I can feel the difference here through the soles of my shoes. The carpet here was both expensive and sound-dampening. Extra security.

At the other end of the hall, three figures are silhouetted in the light from the stairwell. They're not actually *in* the hallway—still on the landing—but I can still hear everything.

My heart goes from zero to fifty—a reaction I couldn't control if I tried.

I've had contracts cry upon delivery. I've had them tremble and shake and beg.

I've never had one fight back.

3

JUSTICE

*I*t takes three of them to drag me up the stairs, and then the third one has to go ahead and push open the door.

Somewhere, deep beneath the fear that I'm going to fucking die right now, I feel a flicker of pride. At least I haven't made it easy. I kick out at goon number one again, but my arms are starting to burn—the tension between their grip and my fight is like holding my hands in a fire. But what's my alternative?

"You can't fucking do this." My shout sinks into what looks like plush carpet as they wrestle me through the door. Clearly, I'm wrong about this. Clearly, they can.

A dark voice whispers that this was bound to happen. That I *deserve* this.

"Feet," the second one says, as if I haven't said anything at all.

"I can't get 'em, are you blind?"

I'm trying to hook my feet around the doorframe to stop them from taking me into this hallway. The second one reaches for my ankles and I push back against the one with his arm locked around my collarbone. I try to dig my heels into the carpet. I make myself heavy.

It doesn't matter.

I lost my shoes a long time ago, though I can't remember when or where. They could be out on that sidewalk corner—I don't know. What I do know is that they've got my hands cuffed in front of me, but not with metal handcuffs. Nothing so fucking pedestrian as that. Padded on the inside, worked leather on the outside, and it doesn't matter how much I try to yank my hands apart. I'll rip my arms apart before the handcuffs break.

With my heels dug into the carpet like this, there is one thing that I can confirm: it's expensive, the pile high enough that whoever owns this place hires someone else to clean it. The walls of the hallway are painted a dusky blue. I twist my body again, pain arcing in my lower back, and catch a glimpse of artwork encased in expensive frames on the walls—flowers in a vase.

All of it is understated in a way that I recognize.

All of it is understated in a way that screams *money.*

One of the goons finally gets hold of my ankle and I pull it back so hard that sharp pain sears up my leg—it's the one I twisted out on the sidewalk.

"Give it up." He doesn't have to say *you little bitch*. It's right there in his tone.

"No."

"Your funeral."

Despite everything—despite the way I throw my weight from side to side, despite the way I slip my ankle out of his hand and aim a kick at his face, the way I shout and scream and thrash—they drag me into a room.

The walls of this room are a flatter, darker blue, so the bench at the center of the wall seems like an optical illusion, the black leather covering flickering in and out of view against the navy.

The sight of it is a truth slamming down like a gate. I've seen benches like that before. In videos. In other people's houses. The kind of thing I'd giggle at behind my hand, heat creeping into my cheeks.

My own mind shoves it away. No. No...

My blood is hot with the missed opportunity. I was supposed to be somewhere else by now. I was supposed to be safe, with Tripp's hand in mine. Anyone's hand in mine, I'm willing to admit, honestly, anyone. We were supposed to be crossing a bridge out of the city, the entire country spread out before us under cover.

Instead I've been kidnapped.

No—not kidnapped. This isn't a kidnapping.

This is a reckoning.

What have I done? What have I *done*?

I'm wearing him out, at least a little—the man with his arms wrapped around me like the worst hug of a lifetime. The other one's guarding the door while I wrestle with the first in a furious, futile battle. He has to be three times my size but I won't quit, won't stop, can't. I kick my heels into the front of his shins and he doesn't flinch. Without high heels, I'm all soft pink flesh, and no matter how much I picture him as a bug to be crushed beneath my heel, I might as well be banging my fists against exposed rock. He's breathing a little faster, though, and my adrenaline-soaked brain seizes on this. The odds are terrible. The odds are insurmountable. But if I can just... keep...fighting...

The man at the door steps aside. I am struggling futilely against my own wrists, against the cuffs.

And then another man steps into the room.

I taste his power the moment he enters—a metallic crackle across the air—and my mind splits neatly in half.

Part of me is still struggling, flailing, anything to get leverage, anything to get away.

And part of me sees nothing but him. *Feels* nothing but him.

His eyes meet mine, but in a breathless rush I realize he's not looking at me, Justice Danes, a woman with choices and an identity and plans other than this. He's assessing. Measuring me up. And there is nothing, *nothing,* in those dark eyes that gives me even a candle's wick of hope.

He lifts one wrist and adjusts a cufflink. The lines of his face are so sharp, so regal. The lines of his suit, the same. And the body underneath that suit is a monument to the kind of manliness that Tripp could never hope to achieve. I can see from here that there's not an inch of softness beneath that suit. Some sick, dark part of me wants to run my fingernails over the hard planes of his muscles, but I know it as clearly as I know the sun will rise—this is the man responsible for my capture.

My *capture.* They stole me off the streets, they threw me in a car, they held me down. It did not matter how much I screamed or protested or threw myself against the locked door. The horror of it sweeps over me in a sweaty cold rush. Monsters. I am in a room full of monsters, and for what? *For what?*

"They'll pay your ransom." I stare into his eyes, I force myself not to look down and away. My mouth is working separately from my body. I am still thrashing. I will never stop thrashing. "They'll pay your fucking ransom, whatever you want."

He looks at me coolly, the hint of something playing at the corner of his mouth, and my stomach sinks like a stone into the ocean. This man, after only seeing this room and the hallway, doesn't need money. He doesn't care about money. I don't think he cares about anything.

The man holding me tightens his grip, compressing his lungs. I'm writhing in his grasp, trying to find any purchase, anywhere.

"You must know by now that this is pointless."

Those are the first words he says to me, the lines of them cutting into my skin even though his tone is absolutely indifferent. He says this in the way that one would say to *grab an umbrella, it's raining out.*

I have to work for the next breath. It comes when I get my feet to make contact with the tops of the man's shoes, and I shove upward. I almost get enough momentum to hit the bottom of his chin with the top of my head, but not quite. Fuck. "What's. Pointless."

He cocks his head to the side and I swear the temperature in the room rises by several degrees. The way his eyes hold me sets me on fire.

"This little display."

I can smell him.

I've been in rooms with a lot of rich men in my life, and not a single one has had power rolling off his skin in waves. Not like this. Not like leather and woodsmoke and a pure metal that has to be dug out of the ground by hand. The scent whips through me like a storm, a cry on the wind—*run, run, run.*

He comes another step into the room and the nearness of him is a lightning strike. I twist and heave against my captor, anything to get away from such raw dominance. The man holding me must feel it, too, because he takes a tiny step backward, squeezing tighter. It squeezes the breath out of me, the last of that pure, sweet oxygen.

Christ. Who is he? *What* is he? And what is he doing here? Dread seeps into every available crevice of my mind. I've heard rumors of a person like him. Hushed ones. The word *arbitration* whispered behind hands, but I never knew why. I thought they were talking about a legal process I'd learned about in one of the prelaw classes I half paid attention to.

Not a person.

Not this man, who is pulling all the air in the room toward himself as if we're past the event horizon of a black hole. No light can escape from its center. No light. Nothing.

My vision is going dark at the edges when he gestures to the man pressing the life out of me.

He lets go.

My knees hit the floor with a crack—here it's thin carpet laid over a hard surface—and I gasp in air that tastes cleaner and fresher than any breath I've ever taken before. Only its tinged with him. It's full of him. Too full for my lungs.

A shadow moves past and disappears out the door, leaving me alone with him. Terror buzzes its way from my fingertips up to the back of my neck.

He removes his jacket, hanging it somewhere out of sight on my next blink. And then he's adjusting his other cufflink.

Not adjusting.

He's rolling up his sleeves.

"Stay on your knees."

The command is so smooth, so easy, that my body begs to obey it. But my mind crumbles under a fresh wave of adrenaline and fear.

I fold up one of my bare feet underneath me, then the other, and push myself to my feet.

And then I spit at his shoes.

4

*M*y blood roars to life in my veins, a tidal rush that threatens to sweep me under and drag me across a rocky ocean floor. The next breath I can force into my lungs feels like the one I'd take if I were crawling up out of the surf, clothes soaked and heavy, making my limbs drag against the sand.

What.

Fucking.

Nerve.

I can feel my entire mind, my entire soul, bending towards her.

In this moment she is the only light left in the universe, and she is a blaze of fire.

Only that flame has been molded into a furious blonde

woman with huge blue eyes and hair that's come partway loose from a neat little clip, making her look feral and post-apocalyptic in the black dress she wears. It glitters in the dim light of the room like it's made of sequins...or diamonds. Something forged through intense pressure and heat.

I know it will burn me to touch her.

I do it anyway.

There is only one answer to the defiance she's thrown at my feet.

I take one step forward as if it isn't there at all and hook my hand through her elbow. She turns instinctively, forgetting for once to fight until I've already taken three more steps, hauling her along with me.

Then she digs in her heels.

I round on her, pulling her as close as I can bear. "You have already made things worse for yourself. You're dangerously close to my limit."

Those blue eyes go even wider and she sets her jaw, but when I tug her forward again she allows it—with minimal resistance. It's token resistance, a token pull of her bound wrists, but I feel it like a burst of electricity through connected wires.

I haul my head above the surface of my shock, of my anger, and my lungs fill with clarity.

I cannot let her do this.

I will *not* let her do this.

She can scream, she can kick, she can fight—but a contract has been signed. I'd wait until morning in any other case. I'd let her wear herself out in the holding cell. But this defiance must be met with an answer.

Now.

The chair in the corner of the room is straight-backed and armless, and the moment I turn toward her, it becomes clear that Justice Danes has no idea what's coming.

Good.

Knowing that—that she's in a moment of hesitation, and fear, if she's smart—sends an icy determination through every one of my veins. It quiets the rush of blood in my ears, slows my heart, sets my jaw.

I sit on the chair and pull her over my lap, her weight clumsily heavy across my legs, bound wrists dangling toward the floor. She rears back, startled, shouting. It likely seems to her that I have snapped, that I have gone beyond all reason, but I am coldly focused as I flip up the back of her dress, exposing a scrap of lace that could charitably be called a thong.

It's not the first curve of flesh I've seen in my life. It's not the first rounded, upturned ass I've seen *today*. But the sight of it, dancing side to side as she shoves herself back and forth, her hip grazing my kneecap...

...the sight of it does things to me.

Unforgivable things.

But no less unforgivable than what she's already done, and she's not the one who's going to run this fucking show.

I tell myself that I'm only looking because it's my responsibility to fulfill this contract, and then I bring my hand down squarely in the center of her right cheek.

The silence is astounding.

I hadn't realized how much noise she was making until she stopped, with a strangled gasp.

I bring my hand down again.

Two bright, red handprints. Matching.

I hardly take any time admiring my handiwork before I give her another set.

By the third, Justice Danes is trying to protest. She's given up her attempts to get away. I have my left arm locked too tightly around her waist for her to go anywhere. Her shock has transformed into a rigid spine. Her head is too high for my taste, making the angle of her ass slightly less than ideal, but it does mean I can hear every sound that escapes her lips.

They are not quite words, not quite whimpers, and all of them tinged with a hot frustration that threatens to crush the lock on the cage around my heart.

As for my cock, it has no such reservations. Not that I can ever let her feel that. Not that I can ever let anyone feel that. I can't even acknowledge it myself. Not now. That would mean throwing away everything I've built, and I won't do it.

Her ass is pink by the fourth set.

Red by the fifth.

By the sixth the muscles of her back give out and her head tips down. She's hanging on by a thread, by the sheer force of her toes gripping the floor, legs pinned together so tightly she's trembling.

Trembling.

It shakes us both.

Seventh.

Eighth.

I got what I wanted.

I have her over my lap, no longer spitting, no longer fighting. I'd call it the first step toward submission, but I have no idea if we're dealing with steps and ladders and progress. Fire doesn't need an invitation to leap from a shorted wire to the rooftop without stopping to take a breath.

My palm is already stinging by the time I deliver the ninth and tenth sets.

The trembling has moved through her entire body now,

rattling the short chain that connects the cuffs on her wrists.

This will be a telling moment.

I half expect her to throw her weight, to leap up and hiss at me like a cat, and my body prepares for it. I'd never do something so obvious as tense while she's still on my lap, but I am intimately involved with every deliberate breath she takes.

Oh, she's trying. She's trying so fucking hard not to act like it affected her, but it did. The back of her neck is pink, right up to where her hair slopes down over her shoulder. And I can feel the tiny hitch in every one of those breaths against my thighs.

The only sound in the room is her breathing.

I give her three more heartbeats to make her escape, and then I rub my hand gently over the handprints I left. It's meant to be businesslike. It's meant to be part of this transaction—the literal finishing touch. But something seizes at the center of my chest when I do it, and again when her body relaxes almost imperceptibly in response.

So imperceptibly that I dismiss it as a fantasy. Emotions like that—anger like that—it's like a drug. The effects don't wear off right away.

Which is how I know it's time for me to exit this little scene and put as much space as possible between me and Justice Danes. I'm going to need the rest of the night to sort out exactly what the fuck is happening here. What Lysander was thinking.

Whether or not I can actually go through with this.

"Up."

Justice lags behind the order for long enough that I have to tap on her shoulder, prompting her. I have half a mind to put her back over my lap, but I can't. The zipper of my pants is on the verge of exploding open, and *that* would end everything.

She stands shakily on her feet, watching me as I stand up, adjust my sleeves and prepare to step outside the room. Among other things, depending on what Justice does.

There's no sudden run for the door, a last dash for freedom. She only stands there in her bare feet, her blue eyes strangely aglow. It's a look I can't place in this room. The fact that her face is so red makes sense, but the look in her eyes squeezes at something low in my gut.

Something I ignore.

Because I'll never throw away my kingdom for a woman. They all go back out the way they came in, justice served.

I snap my fingers and point at the floor next to my feet.

She doesn't understand, and then she does, padding across the space between us to stand next to me. I'd make her crawl, but with her dress still hiked up around her waist, she'll be plenty humiliated as is. It's a good starting point. I'll take her far, far lower while she's here.

"Let's go."

Justice follows me, a half-step behind, out into the hallway and to the left. She doesn't ask where we're going, and when I open the door to the holding cell, she only hesitates a moment before stepping inside.

"Wrists." She holds up her delicate wrists to me, tentative in a way that steals my breath, and I press the hidden switch that releases them. I'll hang them on the rack by the entrance. They'll always be waiting for her.

"We'll begin tomorrow."

There's more I want to ask. There's more I want to say. But wanting doesn't mean doing. Not for me.

I turn to go, but before I can shut the door between us, Justice speaks.

Her voice is just above a whisper. "Who are you?"

I give her the only answer that matters.

"My name is Cassian Locke. But you will call me Sir."

5

JUSTICE

*T*he door shuts behind me, killing the last of the light from the hallway. I rush toward it like I'm still seven years old and afraid of the dark, but there's no light switch on the wall. No touchpad. Nothing.

Of course.

During my search for the nonexistent light switch, my eyes gradually adjust to the dark. It's not pitch-dark, I discover, but the kind of hazy moonlit dark that's clear and unsettling at the same time.

There's not much here.

A low bed, almost a cot, I think, until I go over and find out that it's a platform built into the floor.

I examine it like it's going to give me any information. As if any information could enter my brain at this moment in time. I'm experiencing an insane rush of blood to the

34

head, not to mention the sting of the hotly spanked flesh. Shit—my dress is still pulled up. I tug it back down, cheeks on fire, even though nobody is here to watch.

Or...are they?

I whirl around, searching for the telltale glass of a camera, a small red blinking light—anything.

There's nothing.

Nothing catching any of the moonlit sheen up in the corners of the room.

Still, a shiver moves through me like a wave. The fact that I can't see anything doesn't mean it's not there.

He might not be watching now, but I still feel those dark eyes on me.

And his hands on me.

Heat gathers between my legs and I clap a hand over my mouth, like it could stop me from sucking in a breath. Cassian Locke is like a magnet. I can feel myself pulled back toward him, even though I'm currently locked in...

What is this place, even?

A cell, only a little nicer.

I'm desperate for sensation but tell myself it's not because I liked what happened to me. I can barely face it. Even in my memory. His strong legs underneath me. The clarifying pain of his hand on my ass, over and over and over. Like a naughty little girl.

What the fuck?

It had brought me down from the whirlwind high of the fight, and I'd wanted nothing when it was over so much as I wanted to curl up into his arms and press my face into his neck. Why? *Why?* A rush of pure shame tears the breath from my lips. A man pulled me over his lap to punish me and I can't say I hated it.

Well, I *will* hate it. From now on, I will hate whatever this fucked-up circus becomes.

At the side of the bed, I press my hands down into a thin mattress. It's covered in an equally thin sheet, a thin blanket over top. In the light of the room, it all looks white, and it probably is. White things are easier to bleach.

My heart zigs to the side. Easier to bleach for all the other women who have slept in this room. And there have been other women—I'm sure of it now. I'm sure this is what people like my mother whispered about behind their hands.

People like my mother...and people like my sister.

They'd named her Patience, a throwback if I've ever heard one. Patience, though she was never patient. She was the moon to my sun, dark-haired and pale. A rule-follower, though behind closed doors there were times I saw her rage.

Until she was gone.

Stop thinking of her in the past tense, I tell myself firmly, running the edge of the blanket between my fingers. It *is* flimsy. It would be easy to tear, easy to rip. The fact of it makes my heart thud. It's almost too loud in the silence of the room.

Or...is it really silence?

I strain to hear anything beyond the white noise of the air moving through the room, but it only makes me more aware of that same air coming down from a vent in the center of the ceiling. Every exposed inch of my skin feels its fingertips brushing up against me.

The slightest touch—*air*—and I'm right back over his lap. Part of me wants to shriek and never stop shrieking, and part of me wonders *if this is what happened to Patience...*

It's too hard to consider what this means.

Not about him. Our family might be new money, but I still heard about all the things that people with power do. And maybe it is insane. Maybe it is beyond fucked up that we have a man kidnapping us off the streets in order to...

...in order to what?

My face heats again, hotter this time. Is he the one who decides what people are going to do? Is this man the center of our entire society, one so dark and judgmental that nobody dares utter his name?

The list of my own transgressions seems, here in the dark, really fucking long.

But can that really be what this is about? Making my parents angry? I'm twenty-two. I was on the verge of stepping into my very own life apart from them.

And now...

I have no idea how long this is going to last. Could this have happened to Patience? I pace the length of the cell and turn back around, trying to ignore the hot handprints on my ass. I didn't keep track of her vacations. Why would I? We all have busy schedules, busy lives. If she was gone for...for I don't know how long...

He hasn't said anything about how long he's keeping me here.

Or if he'll ever let me out.

He will, though. Right? He has to. That's not how this is going to work. If people were being murdered, that's— that's a totally different thing. Though I wouldn't put it past him. I wouldn't say he was incapable of it. I felt the power in those hands. He could do anything he wanted.

I pace back across the room and that's when I see it—a narrow door in the center of one wall. My pulse flutters. It can't be this easy. Can it? It could be a trick. All of this could be a little trick to get me in line, and all I have to do now is walk right out of here. In five minutes, I could be blocks away, cursing Tripp for being late. He would deserve a real show, too, me shivering and shaking while he drove around the city trying to find me.

The door opens soundlessly under my hand, and I search for a light switch. My hand brushes against a flat touchpad on the wall, and the dimmest possible illumination shows me exactly what this room is.

It's not a staircase. It's not an exit.

It's a bathroom.

It's barely bright enough to see, and in a color I can't quite identify. It's a strange choice for a man with so much money and power, but then again...it's not strange. Not if they want to control every waking moment. Not if they want to come for me in the night, not risking my eyes having adjusted to the light. I'll always be off guard, as long as I'm here.

They could be coming back any moment now.

I'm overwhelmed with the need to pee, but I do it as fast as I can, heart trapped in my throat, hoping I'll hear them before they come back into the room. There's the world's tiniest sink against one wall, hardly enough room to turn around, and the dark presses in. I've never been claustrophobic, but honestly, this room could do it.

I hurry back out into the relative freedom of the cell.

It's late.

My ass still smarts.

But...there are other feelings, too.

Feelings I won't name, or even acknowledge. Not ever. Not *ever*.

I watch the door for any sign of movement until I have to sit down on the edge of the bed. My feet ache from kicking and fighting, my ankle throbs, and the rest of my muscles are going to follow. I can feel it coming already. But I have to keep watch. What if they catch me while I'm sleeping? Is *that* against the rules, too? What a fucking bastard, leaving me in here with no sense of...anything.

My throat goes tight. I didn't think I'd miss my family, or the penthouse on 32nd Street. And maybe it's not them I miss.

Maybe it's my own freedom.

I let myself fall to the side, my head connecting with a flat, thin pillow. With my head turned to the side, I can still see the faint outline of the door in the wall. That's where they'll come for me. There's no other way in or out. That's what I have to watch. And I'll watch all night if I have to. I'll watch until it's dawn.

6

CASSIAN

"What the fuck were you thinking?"

I find my brother in his rooms, leaned back on his sofa and looking pretty fucking proud of himself. He hasn't even bothered to finish his pour of Johnnie Walker Blue. A snarl rises in my throat. It's a ridiculous habit of his, now that we've brought my father's business back from the brink. Our stability won't last if he has his way about it.

Lysander turns his head toward me with a grin that makes me want to knock his teeth out. "Did you have a nice time?"

The remote—a top-of-the-line thing that's essentially a flat piece of glass—sits on the table next to the sofa. I stab at it hard enough to crack it, but it doesn't give way—the massive television Lysander has been staring at just shuts off.

41

"What. The fuck. Were you thinking?"

He shrugs, putting his glass carefully on the side table. It's a good decision. I *might* fight him right now. That's not out of the realm of possibility. "I took a job, Cash. You can't be pissed at me for that."

"Can't I?" I move around to stand in front of him, forcing him to look at me. It's like looking at myself in a time-lagged mirror. He's three years younger. "We *vet* the jobs we take, Lysander. We don't just accept the money and send out our people."

"It was a good profit."

"You have no idea if she's worth it or not."

My brother raises one eyebrow, and an angry heat spills down my back. "Don't you mean *the contract*?"

I draw myself up to my full height. "*The contract* is unvetted. There's no way you went through the full process while I was finishing up with the previous contract. There wasn't enough time. I don't know what you've gotten us into, and neither do you."

Lysander rolls his eyes and his reply is nonchalant and indifferent. "If it's that big of a deal, just let her go."

"Just let her *go*?" My blood hammers in my veins, and I stab one finger in the direction of his chest, right where his heart is beating, if he has one. "You're the one who came to *me*. Said that she was coming in, like it or not.

This is *your* arrangement." The words hiss from between my teeth.

"Oh, come on, Cash. We both know that every arrangement is *yours*." His mouth twists. "You never let me forget it."

"You want to be an equal partner in running this business? Then stop acting like a fucking child. You don't take a hundred dollar bill from a man on the street without knowing that it comes with a price."

"It doesn't come with a price. Not for me," he says, a snotty edge coating his voice. "For her, maybe."

I change tact. "How did the mediation session go, then? I'm sure you sat down with both parties so they could agree to this as a solution to an ongoing problem, since that's how we do things. Let me see your notes from the session."

His pinched look confirms there was no such session. I've held tens, hundreds of them. That's the only way these things get settled without public court battles and embarrassments. Reputation has always mattered in these circles. The smart families, the families who have made their money last for generations and want to make it last for generations to come, don't want to make the paper for their disputes. There are no public records of what I do, which is the way they like it.

And the way other people like it.

"There are no notes. I think you knew that when you walked in the door."

Anger curdles in my gut, but I keep the lid on it tightly closed. "Everything depends on those sessions. Everything depends—"

"—on discretion," Lysander finishes for me. "I've heard it a million times."

"And yet you accepted this contract with no discretion. With no interview. With *nothing*. Are you not seeing the problem?"

"I'm seeing our bank account." Lysander unfolds himself from the sofa and stands up. One step forward and we're eye to eye. "My focus is on our livelihood. If you want to fight me about it, go ahead."

"Our livelihood only continues if there is absolute discretion. That means no mistakes. That means no fucked-up contracts with someone else's security team."

"You said it yourself. Our people were out there, too."

"Our people were out there without my permission." I've raised my voice, the anger escalating with it, though I only let it show for Lysander's benefit. "Do this again, and you'll be out of the business."

Lines form indents across his forehead. "You wouldn't dare."

"I would dare more than that."

"You need me," he argues. "We'd be several million short if it wasn't for me."

"Several million?" It's an amount. It's like any other amount of money—useless if you can't keep it in the long term. "How long is the contract?"

A satisfied smile lights his face. "*Now* you're asking the right questions."

I put my hands in my pockets, keeping my body absolutely relaxed, and look my brother in the eye. "I've had enough of your shit," I tell him mildly. "If you're going to keep this up, I can arrange for you to be sent back."

He goes still at that, nostrils flaring. The asshole knows what I mean. He knows *where* I mean. He knows as well as I do about the Family that watches us. He's met them in person, and he doesn't want to meet them again. "Five days. Don't be a prick—if our mother were alive to see this—"

"She's not."

Something flares and dies in Lysander's eyes.

"Don't underestimate me." I leave the words at his feet.

Tension tugs at the air between us. Lysander tries his level best, but it's clear my threat has had some impact because his eyes flick to the floor at my feet. It only serves to remind me of Justice Danes, the blazing fire in her eyes, spitting at the floor like a feral woman dragged from the past and fighting for her life.

"I'm going out," he says eventually, then steels himself for one last remark. "Don't wait up."

"I would never," I tell him, the tone dripping with a mixed combination of affection and sarcasm. "Enjoy yourself, Lysander. You deserve it."

He presses his lips together, then takes a silent step around me, heading for the door.

I don't wait up for him—that much was true. But I don't go to sleep, either.

Alone, the thought of her fills the room, and the hallway, and my own rooms.

I settle in front of the secure laptop that gives me access to all our records. We're tax paying citizens, another fact that would surprise the newly flush entrepreneurs who think that avoiding this responsibility is the key to making a fortune. It's not. Paying taxes is the equivalent of hiding in plain sight. The government might frown upon the kind of extrajudicial private arrangements I facilitate, but they'll never have a reason to investigate so long as they get their due.

I try not to think of Justice Danes another moment as I pull up the record.

It's a fucking mess.

Lysander did more than avoid the mediation session that I always insist on before accepting contracts. The amount is recorded, and it is a high one, but the rest of the information doesn't make any sense. The money has come directly from the Danes Family Trust. There is no other party involved in the dispute, but there must have been one, because the instructions are clear:

Break her.

Someone wants her brought to heel.

There's more attached to the document, but it's information on Justice, not the dispute. There are photos of her taken from a long-range lens, dancing in a club. There's a man in many of the photos, tall and blonde, with his mouth on hers. More photos—the two of them in a private home.

The sight of his hands on her makes my insides flare with jealousy.

I acknowledge the feeling and then dismiss it entirely. I have been in the company of Justice Danes for less than an hour. There is no reason I should be interested in her at all. There's no reason I should give a fuck that this mystery man had his hands on her as recently as...

...last night.

It takes one shove to get myself clear of the desk. The floor-to-ceiling windows in my main room provide a stunning view of the city, and though I look out over all the buildings, all the twinkling lights, I don't see any of it.

Something seethes in my blood. She's different. She's different from all the rest.

Either that, or I've passed my limit for the day. I don't allow myself to have feelings for or about the contracts. That's what it means to be a neutral party. That's why I am trusted among the richest families in the city—in the world. My name is making its way across the oceans. There is only more money, more quiet success, to come if I can keep my shit together.

I've never had a problem with it before.

There's nothing for me to see out the window, so I stalk through the process of getting ready for bed.

I'm still lying there, awake, thinking of her, when my assistant Jeannine raps lightly at the doorframe. It's been hours. It's been all night.

"Good morning," she says softly.

I only have one thing to say.

"Prepare her."

7

"*I*t's time to get up."

I push myself upright on the mattress, blinking into the light streaming in from the hallway. It's not just light from the hallway, actually, but there's light coming through the high, thin window, too.

Shit.

The woman stands framed in the doorway, the light from the hall equalizing the sunlight filtering in from the window. I swipe my hands over my eyes, trying to feel less...less trapped. It doesn't work. No matter how well I can see, I'm still equally trapped. My heart speeds up.

"Okay. Okay." Whoever this woman is, she's tall and gorgeous and looks completely impassive. "I'm awake."

"No," she says with a hint of impatience in her voice. "It's time to get up. We need to prepare you."

"Prepare me?"

She cocks her head to the side. "Did you think you'd serve out your contract in some club dress and last night's makeup?"

"I—" I'm tangled up in the blanket, which is more the consistency of a sheet. Somehow, even though I woke up in the same position I fell asleep, it's wrapped around my waist, pinning me to the bed. I have to twist around to free myself, conscious of the woman's eyes on me every moment. "I don't know. I've never been kidnapped before."

"You haven't been kidnapped." Her voice is low and melodic, and I half wonder if she could hypnotize me. Snap her fingers. Wake me up in my own bedroom. "You're here under contract."

"Contract? What does that—" I interrupt myself with a final, vicious yank at the blanket, which finally frees me from its grasp. There's no choice but to plant my bare feet on the cold floor and stand, which has the unfortunate effect of revealing to both of us that my skirt is also hiked up around my waist. The blanket probably tugged it there, the sick fuck. I try not to care as I pull it back down, but a strange heat lashes itself across my cheeks. Who *am* I? Last night, I was a woman who kicked and screamed and fought, and this morning I'm—

They might have control over me. They might be able to...prepare me. And punish me. And kill me, though I try very hard not to entertain that idea. But they're not going to shame me.

I force myself to look into her eyes. She really is stunning, with huge dark eyes and dark hair twisted back into an elegant knot behind her head. Looking at her this way might be brave, but it also makes me painfully aware that I look like a complete wreck. I don't have to touch my hair to know that it's a mess, fought in and slept on and otherwise rumpled, and my skin has a nervous film coating it.

Disgusting.

"Wrists," she says, and tips her head toward the door. Her tone is even but it's an order if I've ever heard one.

"What's your name?"

She takes in a little breath. "Mika. But you will never call me that."

In the end, I won't be able to overpower her. I know from last night that she has a cadre of burly men at her fingertips. I lift my chin. There are small ways to defy someone. Tiny ways, like hesitating for a heartbeat too long. That's what I do before I move across the room toward her, then present my wrists.

I thought I was the one who was better at this game, but when I've taken the last steps, she's still looking at me. Her gaze reminds me of Cassian Locke, which sends a mortifying warmth rocketing out from my core to my fingertips. Are they...related? Or has he just bestowed some power on her that makes me weak in the knees?

"You can drag your feet if you want to," she says coolly, "but everything you do will be reported to Mr. Locke."

"And?" I don't feel brave, but I make myself sound like it. "What then? What's the worst that could happen?" I laugh out loud at the absurdity of this warning. "You've already taken me off the streets. He's already...spanked me." I force the words out even though they taste like lust and shame. "I'm at rock bottom."

"Oh, no, Ms. Danes. You still have a long way to go."

The cryptic warning hovers in the air above us while she fastens the cuffs to my wrists, then attaches a chain to some hidden loop in the cuffs. I have to bite my lip to keep from making a caustic comment about how it's not good manners to treat a guest like a dog, but I remember last night's punishment. I still feel it. And if I'm going to survive this, it's probably best to choose my battles.

I don't even know if this *is* one of the battles I should be fighting.

It takes her a solid tug on the chain to get me to walk behind her, and when she turns, all I can see in her eyes is that she's put one more tally on her list. Part of me is proud. Part of me shivers. But all of me, in the end, follows her down the hall. She turns a corner into a narrower hallway, leading me down to a door on the right.

It opens into a light-soaked room that looks part locker room, part sterile salon. Two other women wait inside, wearing black uniforms. They size me up as I'm led into the room. Part of me wants them to see how unbroken I am. Part of me wants to crawl underneath what's clearly a waxing table. My heart throws itself jaggedly against my rib cage. This could turn out to be a nasty scene, if they want, and here I am, being led around on a chain.

Things happen fast after that.

Under Mika's cool guidance, the other two come forward. One brandishes a pair of scissors, and I can't help it—I shrink back toward the door.

The first woman pulls sharply on the chain. "None of that. Step forward and spread your legs."

The second one has *scissors,* so this time I don't hesitate, though my stomach curls with embarrassment. And why? Why should I be embarrassed? They're doing this to me. I'm just trying to stay alive.

"Hold still."

I stare straight ahead until the woman gives another yank on the chain. "*Yes, mistress,*" she says.

The words stick in my throat, but then again...scissors. "Yes, mistress."

"That's a good girl."

Good girl. It sparks something dirty in the back of my

mind, something that makes my mouth water. God. What the fuck is wrong with me?

They cut my clothes off of my body.

That's what the scissors are for.

It's deliberate and dispassionate and it makes me feel smaller with every piece they shred. The dress goes first, then my bra, and then with a final *snip* they tug off the thong that's underneath.

The other three women appraise me. I'm trying desperately not to cover myself. I'm trying desperately to remember that I'm proud. But it's like they cut off part of my resolve when they cut into that fabric.

"Shower," Mika commands, and I force myself to think of her as "mistress" as she leads me to a shower stall around one corner. They choose the water temperature, the water spraying down full force, and then she pulls my chain through a loop in the ceiling and forces my arms over my head.

I am not even allowed to bathe myself. They do it. Roughly. The commands come one after the other. *Spread your legs. Turn around. Face up. Bend forward.* For this last bit, the chain loosens a couple of inches. They make me turn under the spray, my body shuddering with goosebumps. One of them turns off the water abruptly, and then they towel me dry while my teeth chatter.

Mika comes close when she takes the chain from the loop, and I summon my courage and look her in the eye.

"Why are you doing this?" I ask, my voice distorted by the chattering. "You don't have to do this." The last bit comes out as more of a plea than I wanted it to.

For the first time, while she's holding the chain that binds me, Mika shows a hint of pity. "Oh, you precious thing," she says. "You're not here to be ransomed. You're here to be punished."

I don't know what to say to that. Her words make a thousand questions bloom in my mind, but from the brisk way she leads me over to the waxing table, I can tell that the conversation is over.

They make me get up onto the table, only I don't have a shirt or a little paper sheet to give me the illusion of modesty. She lets a little slack into my chain so that I can tug my knees up to my chest. I don't hesitate to do that, because I have never been so exposed, and if this is about punishment, then I'm not starting with this. He can punish me later, if he wants, but now? No. No...

It's not until they start spreading the wax that I realize this is all part of it. Every bit.

"Hold still, precious thing," she says. "Three, two, one."

8

*M*ika presents her to me at noon so we can begin the first day of the contract. It seems that Justice has already learned at least one lesson from last night and the efforts of this morning, and I'm partly relieved and partly disappointed. I would have liked to wrestle her down into position. It's one of my most shameful thoughts. This want is not something I can ever entertain, so the more submissive she is, the easier this will be...for both of us.

She's led into the room on the end of Mika's chain, her eyes on the ground.

I almost have to walk out.

The words rise in my throat—*stop this, I can't do this, this is too dangerous for both of us*—but, like every other emotion, I swallow them down.

The fact is that Justice Danes was a masterpiece in that

ridiculous sequined dress. She made me hard for her, twisting and turning and fighting against the ad-hoc recovery team. I spent all night willing myself not to take myself in my own hand—anything for release. I didn't, because I can't. Because I'm stronger than that.

And maybe I could have been stronger than Justice Danes in her little club outfit. I could have contained myself if I had only seen her perfect ass exposed.

But now she's naked.

Mika has followed the protocol down to the last detail. I can tell with a single sweep of my eyes. Justice's nails have been buffed and polished. Her skin has been scrubbed to a soft sheen. Her hair has been carefully dried and styled in a low bun at the nape of her neck that won't interfere with any of my plans.

And her pussy is bare.

It's still a little pink from the waxing, and the sight of that cleft between her legs is like dynamite exploding into bedrock. An aftershock, then another—I didn't get to see the rest of her body before. The lift of her breasts. The curve of her waist into her hips. Miles and miles of exquisite skin. A birthmark on her hip the color of hot chocolate. I want to lick it. I want to do more than that. Far more than that. And I want her on her knees. Oh, fuck me, I want—

Mika tugs on the chain and Justice takes another step into the room. At that moment she raises her eyes from the floor and looks into mine, and the shock that goes through me is more than an earthquake. It's fucking celestial.

I've never seen anything like it. I've never seen so much hate and so much need and so much confusion in one person's eyes. It's true that the people I see in this room are no more than their contracts—I don't bother looking into their eyes to see their feelings, unless I need to know that they have adequately paid the price for their behavior.

They're so blue. Blue like the sky. Blue like the sea. Shifting in color. I only let the murkiest daylight into this room, from windows high up on the wall to match the holding cell. They're tinted, the light filtered. I want them to know this is all part of the contract from the light, and from the look on her face, Justice knows.

I cannot hesitate.

I can only pretend that these heartbeats I've spent drinking her in are a regular part of the process. Mika doesn't let it show in her expression, but she must feel that something is off. It wouldn't be so odd, in this moment, to discover that my heart is bleeding through my shirt.

Ignore it.

Ignore it.

Mika clears her throat. "The contract, sir."

It snaps me back into reality with a tumble of anticipation that I never feel. All those things I want to do to Justice begin here. This way. With punishment. As long as I'm touching her, none of the rest matters. I make the compromise with myself knowing that it's a deal with the devil.

"Put her over the bench."

Two high, pink spots appear on Justice's cheeks, but she bites her lip and says nothing as Mika leads her across the room and to the bench, with its spaces for arms and legs and cuffs and chains. Mika gives a yank to Justice's chain. "Up."

I see the set of her jaw, the little lift of her chin. There's a defiant spark in her eyes. Well. She might have a spark, but there's an ice storm in my gut, ready to crush it.

My breath must be colder than the air when I finally let it out. I can't go into this session like that. I can't. But the more I try to shove it down, the more the snow creeps upward, filling my torso.

"Up," Mika warns again.

I double what I had planned for Justice. This is only the first day. And on the first day, our focus will be on punishment for past behavior. It helps that every moment she hesitates is ticking solidly into the past. My blood rushes through my veins like a freight train.

Justice must be exploiting the self-doubt that Mika has worked so hard to excise from herself, and once again, the world shifts beneath my feet. There's nothing on Mika's face that gives this away, but I do feel it in the air.

"Leave her to me."

Mika flashes me a look of pure relief, then gets herself under control. She drops the chain into my hand and floats out the door with her head held high, pulling it shut behind her. The soft *click* it makes when it shuts is barely audible, but Justice whips her head in that direction.

"Obedience is your only option." I pull the chain so that she has to move directly behind the paddling bench.

The tension that comes through the chain isn't metaphorical. It's physical, and I feel it like it's hooked into my own chest.

I don't let her see the way it makes me feel.

I don't let her see that it makes me feel at all.

I only look at her like she's a little brat, and I have all the power. Because, I remind myself, that is exactly our circumstance.

"Obedience is your only option, and it also has the virtue of being your best option."

Justice looks at me from underneath her eyelashes. "If that's what you think."

I clench my hand, the one hidden from her view, into a fist, then release it. "You're so quick to forget the rules."

"If that's what you think, *sir.*" Something adjacent to a smile plays over her mouth. It's fucking unbelievable. The closer she gets to trouble, the more she seems to love it.

Last night was only a taste. It was a shadow of what's to come.

"You'll soon find that it's the truth."

She lets out a breath that's like a little sigh. "No, sir."

I stare at her until she looks up from the paddling bench and into my eyes. When she does, the brave facade slips a little bit. I consider her like she's a science project. "Are you trying to make things worse for yourself?"

Justice straightens her back, which has the intoxicating effect of putting her breasts on full display. "I don't see how things *could* get any worse for myself. I'm here to be punished for a crime—I assume it's a crime—I didn't commit. I've been stripped. I've been waxed. I've been—"

"The only thing that matters now is what *will* happen to you." I increase the tension on the chain, which forces her to lean back on her heels. She tries to hide it. It can't be disguised. "So you can play your little games. You can resist. You can scream and shout and beg. But none of that will spare you."

"I'm not trying to be spared," she says, a jagged edge in her voice. "I'm trying to fuck with you." My chest goes tight and cold. "And it's totally working. It might not show on your face, but I know. Deep inside, you—"

I tie the chain off to a loop on the wall and leave it stretched tight.

And then I reach for my tie.

I tug it off in one smooth motion.

It's enough to get Justice's attention. "Deep inside—"

It takes me three steps to move behind her, and then she struggles. She pulls uselessly at the cuffs, but the chain is strong. It holds. And before she can fall to the floor, or tilt to the side, I wrap my arm around her and press her back to my chest as hard as I can.

Justice sucks in a breath, which gives me the opportunity to gag her with the tie. Once it's securely around the back of her head, I run my fingers across the sumptuous fabric, already hot from her ragged breath.

There. *Now* she looks afraid.

"Scream all you want," I tell her, and then I lift her bodily up onto the paddling bench and strap her down. "You'll need to."

9

JUSTICE

I am bound and have no escape. His expensive tie tastes like sin in my mouth, and my blood rages against my veins as I fight against the bonds cutting into my wrists. It runs ice cold one moment, burning like fire the next. I'm overwhelmed by terror one moment and consumed by a sense of power in the next. I cannot get a handle on which feeling will overtake me next.

The adrenaline surging through my veins is almost painful, sharpening every sensation. I open my eyes wider, as if seeing the details of this room in stark relief, seeing all of its details and imperfections, can help me escape. I jerk my wrists and ankles against the ties binding me to the bench, over and over, but the effort is futile.

I try to escape.

But there is one humiliation that I can't possibly admit to him—me, the girl who spit at his feet.

And that is the fact that some small, terrible, filthy part of me *wants* this. *Craves* this.

Why does it feel so fucking good to be strapped down like this and stripped of all my agency? Why does it feel so pure, this moment, with my ass poised in the air and my pussy on full display? The air circulating through the room reminds me of how exposed I am every single moment. It reminds me that he could expose even more of me, and I would be powerless to stop him.

I suck in another ragged breath through the crumpled fabric of his tie as he positions himself next to me. The space around him seems to heat up. He's pissed. I won that battle, at least—I got a rise out of him. I know it even if he won't admit it. And why would he? He's Cassian Locke, and I'm no one. An ass to be punished. But I can feel it in the air like you can feel a cold front whipping across the city, block by block.

"Forty strokes. For your disobedience."

He's crazy. He's fucking *crazy*. He brought me here and told me what to do, and *now* he thinks he can punish me for not listening to him? What did he expect when he had his people drag me up all those flights of stairs—that I would just lay down and take it?

I buck against the bonds, trying fruitlessly to get free as my brain computes exactly what that means—forty strokes. He does not have a light hand, Cassian Locke. Not at all. My previously spanked flesh still smarted this morning when I woke up. This has to be worse. There's no question about it.

The first strike lands without warning, in a blaze of heat and a pain that feels white, then red, and then smolders as his hand comes down on the other side. Again, again, again. It doesn't matter that I pull at my wrists and shout incoherently into the tie. The blows are as inevitable as the sunrise and the sunset, and my ass is its own sun. It's on fire, like embers about to explode into flame.

The first ten land, fifteen, twenty, and he has not varied his rhythm, as if he wants to show me how relentless he can be. Well, he has shown me. I can feel it rocketing through every inch of me. It would make my teeth knock together if they weren't held hostage by his tie.

All at once, it ends.

I find myself heaving in labored breaths through the tie, my entire body trembling. All my focus is on the searing pain in my flesh. It pulls my mind away from every other sensation.

Except...the *craving*.

As the moments tick by, I become aware of another humiliating fact.

I'm rocking back and forth on the bench, as much as my bound wrists and ankles will allow. It isn't much, and it's certainly not enough to allow my clit to gain any traction on the leather surface, but oh, my God, this is what I have become.

It takes all the effort in the world to hold still, but my face feels as red as my ass must be. And there's no way he could have missed those movements.

Could he?

I hold as still as I can, though I'm still trembling, praying somehow that I will fade into the black leather bench and disappear.

Instead, he offers proof that he can, in fact, see me.

It's a steady hand on the reddened flesh, and it's rubbing in slow circles. I can tell that it's not meant to be comforting—he's testing me. I want to press back into it more than I've ever wanted anything. Not because more pressure will feel *better*, but because it will feel at all, send another spike of pure sensation ricocheting through me.

Cassian Locke does not offer any congratulations for surviving his onslaught, or even a comment. He rubs first one cheek, then the other, pressing different spots with his fingertips. It seems impossible to be so attuned to his touch when it's a burning expanse of skin, but I feel every touch.

I also feel the desire building between my legs, and a horrified thought pops into my mind. What if I'm wet? What if I'm leaking onto the bench? What if he sees *that* when he lets me up?

He should let me up any moment now, and I wriggle a bit in my restraints, trying to encourage him. He's punished me. He should let me go back to my room—my cell.

His hand lifts away from my skin, and I wait for him to come around to release my wrists.

His footsteps moving behind me make my heart sink.

There's a clink of metal somewhere in the corner of the room. His footsteps approach, and then a strip of black leather swings into my vision, dangling from his hand.

It's a belt.

The sight of it deposits a cold, twisting fear in the pit of my gut, along with something else I can't explain and can't begin to process right now. I only know that this is going to be worse. *This* is something to be afraid of.

All of my soul curls around the silence in the room. All of my mind goes with it.

I can't see him. I can't read his eyes, or even guess what he's thinking, but as the moment draws out, I swear I feel...hesitation.

That feeling splinters and shatters on the ground when he voices his next words.

"Four strokes."

Four. It's possible I'll hate the number four for the rest of my life. Or maybe, shamefully, I'll love it. I give one last tug at my arms, at my ankles, and I am still bound. And again, I am reminded that there's no way out.

I tense, waiting for the belt to land, and that's when Cassian Locke laughs.

I've never heard such a dangerous laugh. How can his voice be so smooth, yet so barbed, at the same time? It makes me hotly furious. Furious that he's laughing at me. Furious that a part of me likes this. No—it's not as simple as that. I *hate* it, but I *need* it.

I'm completely helpless to say anything, so I have to wait for him, feeling his power throbbing through the room with every breath he takes.

"Do you think I'll dispense this punishment just like that?" He traces a finger down the small of my back, and I automatically arch for him, falling deeper into that abject humiliation, an embarrassment I don't think I'll be able to forget for the rest of my life. "Not while you're fighting me. I'll wait as long as it takes."

"Why?" I retort, the word completely garbled by the tie.

"It's not enough that you bear it," he says, as if this is obvious. "The punishment is in the offering."

The words ring in my head, turning over and over, folding back in on themselves, and somehow they've caught my attention. I don't want to offer myself to him. I don't. *He* brought me here. I didn't choose to come here. My own answers come fast and hard and they are all lies, lies to the core.

Because I can feel my body responding to him. To the scent of him in the air. To the space he fills as if he owns it, as if he owns *me*, and in this moment he does. The wet heat pooling between my thighs is proof enough of that.

The battle rages. Mind and body, back and forth, one over the other, a whirlwind.

And in that whirlwind, I forget.

Forget to be tense, to brace myself for the inevitable lash of pain, the stripe of fury that will fall whether I want it to or not. I forget. I am supposed to be endlessly vigilant, I am supposed to delay this as long as possible, I am supposed to fight until the bitter end.

But I forget.

"Good girl."

The words stab into the center of my mind, a shock that brings me back to myself—wait, *wait*—

The belt comes down across my ass, a bright-white pain leaving a thick band. He's caught me off-guard. I can't stop the strangled scream that rumbles in my throat but is hushed by the tie. I can't stop the tears.

"One," he counts.

10

I need distance. I need air. I need light.

In the hall I snap my fingers for Mika, who will take her back to the cell and administer any necessary care. It will only be soothing to a point. It will only be kindness for a fleeting moment. The purpose is to make her ready for tomorrow's session. That's all.

I should have stayed to reinforce the lesson I was trying to teach, when the even lines of the belt were imprinted on her skin. It would have been according to every protocol I've established for myself over the last five years.

I've built them up so fucking carefully, so meticulously, these rules. And yet I stood there afterward, holding that belt in my hand, breathing hard.

So was Justice, through the tie I'd gagged her with. My own tie from around my own neck. That was when it started—when I took off my *own* tie, part of my uniform, part of my *armor*—and used it to silence her. God, they were delicious, those sounds she made through the cloth.

It woke me up.

I had been sleeping, but now I am fully, painfully, horribly awake.

The housekeeper shies out of the way when she sees me coming. I feel like I must be thundering, my footsteps loud, but this place isn't meant to amplify anyone's comings and goings. That's how my father liked things. Discreet and quiet, unless he was in the room with a contract. Then they were as loud or as quiet as he liked.

And never once did I see him react to a contract this way. Not *once*. That has always been the guiding principle of this work: never get involved. Never get attached. Never get emotional.

I don't know if lust is an emotion, but it has completely taken me over.

My cock is throbbing, leaking, and it's all I can do to keep myself from breaking into a run.

I'm almost to my room when Lysander saunters out of his, a delighted sneer twisting his face. "Poor Cassian. Did you overexert yourself? I can tell by the look of you that—"

"Fuck off." His shoulder gives under the palm of my

hand, a push meant to toss him out of my way. It sends him back a couple of steps, and his eyebrows raise.

"What did she do *this* time? Spit in your face?"

I wheel on him then, my breath too harsh and heavy for my lungs. Once, twice, I try to steady myself. "You have no idea what you've done."

He crosses his arms over his chest, arrogant to the fucking last. "Looks like *you're* the one who's in over *his* head."

"I have a call."

"Enjoy." He gives me a jaunty wave.

"You'll wait for me in the den."

"Oh? Will I?"

I bite back the urge to let loose a string of profanities. My brother, more than anyone alive on the planet, knows how to get under my skin. All I can do is consider it practice for when I'm in the room. One deep breath in, one deep breath out. "Yes. Before this goes any further, I need more information about the contract."

He rolls his eyes toward the ceiling, looking for an instant exactly like he did as a petulant teen. "I gathered all the pertinent information."

"You did not, and we both know it. The den. Half an hour."

"I have an engagement, which you'd know if you cared to ask—"

"Cancel it. Postpone it. Whatever you have to do. We have business matters to discuss, and if you can't be available..." I lift one shoulder in a shrug that I hope telegraphs *"then I'll kick you to the fucking curb, you asshole, and I'll see to it that you never come back here."*

He's opening his mouth to protest when I turn away, taking the last few steps to the door of my suite.

"Cassian—" I slam the door on him and flip the lock. Then I key in the code on the separate security system I installed when ownership of the property was transferred to me. Nobody is coming through that door now.

I press my back against it. The door, at least, is solid. It's not a modern pressboard piece of shit. It's not hollow... like I am.

Like I *was*.

What is it about her that's made me this way? She's beautiful. Of course she's beautiful. Most of the women who come here, either as pawns in someone else's deal or to pay for their own sins, have had a lifetime of practice enhancing their beauty. But even with Mika's simplest makeup, Justice shines.

She's like an avenging angel.

One that's so powerful in her fury, yet delicate enough that I can bind her and bend her.

Whether I can break her is another question entirely.

That's one of the things that makes my heart race. I might've gone too far today. It's always been part of my protocol that I start simply, building up to peak severity at the end. That's what the payers expect, and that's what I deliver.

But, somehow, she got to me.

She burrowed her way under my skin, to the gilded cage that rests around my heart, and she melted it with the heat of her words.

It was impressive, how long she fought. And it was more impressive how she bore the punishment I gave her. It *was* too much. The belt? On the first day? She'd challenged me, and instead of remaining in control, I'd accepted.

And then...

And then...

I shove myself away from the door. My clothes feel too tight, too constricting, and I strip them off piece by piece. Jacket. Shirt. Belt. It wasn't my belt that I used on her—it was the one that hangs in that room expressly for that purpose—but to touch it is to cause the memory to flood back as if it's happening all over again.

Her tears were fascinating in a way that no other woman's tears have been. I wanted to lick them off her face.

And then I wanted to lick all the way down her body to that sweet space between her legs.

I leave a trail of clothing on the way to my bathroom, shoving the handle on the shower so hard I'm surprised it doesn't come off in my hand. The stream is instantly powerful, on the verge of scalding, and I throw myself under it like it has any hope of cleansing me. It would be holy water if I could wish it so.

The end.

The end was when I knew that nothing about Justice Danes was going to be the same. This was no neat and tidy contract, and it never would be.

Because she wanted it.

When the leather of the belt lifted away from her skin for the last time, she was no longer holding still. Her body shook with little whimpers, and for a moment I was relieved. It had been so easy. Almost *too* easy.

I was fucking right.

Justice wasn't squirming away from the belt. It took one heartbeat for that to be clear. She was rocking her hips forward, straining to get herself off against the surface of the bench. The noises coming from her throat weren't cries of defeat. They were cries of desire.

I dropped the belt to the floor, and she turned her head at the sound, still moving, still trying to find release.

Her blue eyes had locked on mine.

She was a gloriously pathetic sight. Naked, my tie soaked in saliva from being lodged between her teeth. Fighting to rub her clit against the bench I'd bent her over to teach her a lesson.

I turned away from her to hide how much I wanted to give her more.

One last little whimper emerged from around the tie. It sounded so much like *please.*

I'd gone.

Mika waited in the hall, and I'd gone past her with a brusque, "Take her back."

Here, under the hot water, I can give myself over to it.

I wrap my fist around my hard length and pull and pull and pull while the water lashes my own back, running hot and bright down the backs of my legs, the sensitive creases of my knees, and the hard tendons at my ankles. It's so hot it hurts. It's penance and it's pleasure, all at once.

"Fuck," I grunt. "*Fuck.*" The impending orgasm builds, drawing my balls up tight. I came in here to get her out of my head, but I can't. My mind is frantic to remember every inch of her. The reddened flesh of her ass. The pink, glistening folds of her pussy. And that particular rock of her hips, back and forth, back and forth, searching for a sensation she could never have while she was restrained like that.

Unless I gave it to her.

The mental image of sliding my fingers between those legs to collect that sweetness sends me over the edge, into a roaring orgasm I don't bother to stifle. All of me empties into the center of the shower, one arm braced against the wall and the other engaged in this futile attempt to forget.

I watch the fruits of my efforts swirl down the drain as I try to catch my breath.

Then I reach for the soap.

It's time to meet my brother.

11

*E*very minute seems like an eternity. They are all small eternities, folding in on themselves and exploding back outward. They crash against the blank walls of my cell and echo back on me, a tightening spiral of shame.

My own fury tastes like desire.

It shouldn't taste like this, shouldn't feel like this. The anger I feel should be a wall that keeps the thought of Cassian Locke from touching me.

But the memory does touch me.

I could blame the fact that I'm locked in a cell with nothing to do, but the more I stare at that too-high slit of a window, the more I know that the cell is blameless.

It's me who is ruined.

Two days with Cassian Locke, and I am *ruined.*

I squeeze my eyes shut in the half-light of the cell and try to remind myself that Tripp exists, somewhere on this planet. At least—I think he does. They took my phone, obviously, so there is no way for me to contact him and find out what happened. What on earth could have kept him from picking me up?

The brutal truth is that there are any number of things Tripp could have chosen over me. A party. A dinner. God forbid he let the plan slip in any way to one of his sisters, or his mother. They'd have his head for that. My stomach goes cold at how perfectly stupid I was with him. He was convenient and his own stupidity clearly dragged me down. I saw him as an escape hatch. He saw me as a liability.

Or maybe they got him, too.

And honestly, I don't find myself caring. Not much. Not enough.

I sit on the edge of my bed and drop my head into my hands. If anything happened to him, it's my fault. There's no way around that. I convinced him to go away with. I planned and schemed and brought him along every step of the way.

I wanted to be free, and I walked right into a trap.

You didn't care about him, an evil little voice whispers in the back of my mind. And you liked what happened to you today.

"No." My voice bounces back at me. The echo seems louder than when I spoke, which should be impossible. "I didn't like it," I whisper.

Two days with Cassian Locke. I can't be coming apart already, can I? Or is one punishment session—God, I can't believe I'm thinking of them this way, as set in stone, as set in my schedule—all it takes to push me over the edge?

The truth about how I feel is so slippery it makes me feel filthier than I already do, with that sheen of sweat still on my skin and the wetness lingering between my legs. I didn't like it.

I hated it.

And I craved it.

I still crave it now. Even now, after I was brought back here with cuffed hands and a sore ass. Mika made me lay on my stomach and rubbed some kind of cream into my skin. It made it feel better. A little.

But it didn't wipe the thoughts from my mind.

Filthy thoughts.

The groan comes from somewhere deep inside me, a strangled noise filled with wanting. Until today, nobody has ever restrained me. Until today, nobody has ever spanked me. I've never been belted. That's not how things worked in our world. There was decorum.

That decorum, I remind myself fiercely, was a veneer for

the kinds of nasty secrets I couldn't bear to keep any longer.

Is it so bad that I used Tripp as a means to an end, if it meant I could build a life safe from those secrets? If, one day, I could work to cleanse my family's past of all those dark and terrible corners?

It was not something I could do from inside the house.

The thought strikes like lightning. Cassian could have been involved in that. More intimately involved than I ever knew. How else would his people know where to find me? How else could he be so confident that my punishment is deserved?

I can't focus on these arguments.

To think of any of them is to think of Cassian. To think of Cassian is to remember how exposed I was, bent over that strange bench, my wrists and ankles bound. It's to remember the way his hand came down on my flesh without hesitation.

It's to remember the burn.

That burning pain spreading over every inch of me, around the front of my hips and between my legs and that part of me cried out in recognition.

It was what I've always needed. I've been asking for years, I see now.

I grit my teeth and let myself fall back on the pillow. I am still naked. Mika didn't even bring me a robe. She uncuffed my hands and left without another word. The sheets press coolly against my punished ass.

I can't let it come to this. I can't give in this way. Cassian Locke is a monster, and I'm *not*. I'm not. And only a complete fucking freak would like what he did to me. Only a complete freak would squeeze her eyes shut and shove a knuckle in her mouth to quiet her little noises. Only a nasty, dirty freak would slip her hands down below her waist and between her legs, teasing the clit that had been so desperate for attention when the pain was fresh and hot and endless.

I arch back against the sheets, circling that swollen, aching bundle of nerves with my fingertips. Relief battles with frustration. I'm oversensitive, aware of every inch of my skin. *Too* aware. The fine edge between pleasure and pain dances back and forth, forcing me to chase it.

Cassian did this to me.

I *hate* that he did this to me.

But that hatred—it feels so alive, so essential, that I want to bottle it up and drink it every night. It's a dark energy that thrums through my veins along with my heartbeat, straight to that space between my legs that aches and wants and fights.

Why can't it be easy? Why can't it be easy to get myself off? I try not to think of him. I try not to think of the way his suit moves with his body. I try not to think of the way his dark eyes rake over my skin like I'm a piece of property.

I try to think of anything else. Another man. Tripp. *Any* other man. But the men in my imagination are the equivalent of cold, boring water, stagnant at the bottom of the tub. They're a safe bet and I want nothing to do with them.

None of them have ever caused me any pain. Or if they did, it was superficial—fake the way that soap operas are fake. It only ever went skin deep and it wasn't hot enough to make my core coil up in pleasure and frustration.

Cassian forces his way back into my mind, and my body responds like he's standing in the room with me. I can't help the little whimper that escapes my throat, because as much as I hate him, I wish he *was* standing in the room with me. A voice in the back of my mind whispers that if he's so skilled at delivering pain, he must also be skilled at delivering pleasure. I know it deeply, down into my bones, though I've never once thought of it before. It makes abundant, cosmic sense. He holds the key to both pain and pleasure in the palm of his hand. Each is impossible without the other.

I don't want to be lying here in this bed on my back.

I guiltily and desperately want to be back splayed on that bench. Anything—I'd take anything. A vibrator pinned beneath me. A punishment in progress. Anything. But there is no other furniture aside from this boxy bed, this thin mattress, and so I have to settle for bending over it.

This has to be the neediest I've ever looked, one hand fisted in the thin sheets and one down in the hot, wet crease between my spread legs.

There is no choice in the matter. I have to think of Cassian, or lose the orgasm that threatens.

And so I do.

I imagine him in this small, cramped space, standing behind me. He'd disapprove—I know he would—but yet a certain heat would be present in his eyes as he watched. Would he let himself touch me? No. He will only allow himself to be provoked as long as it serves him.

He would remain in total control. He would hold that over me without laying a finger on my skin.

Do it, precious thing, he'd whisper to me in that dark, sinuous voice of his. Make yourself come, bent over your bed like the whore that you are. Spread those legs for me. Wider. I want to see more of you. I want to watch while you debase yourself for an orgasm. If I stop you, will you beg? How prettily will you beg me if I tie those wrists together and chain them over the wall so you can't reach that aching clit? Oh, how you like this. You love this. You need it. You crave it.

I pant breathlessly against the sheets, my mouth open, a prayer on my lips: thank God no one is here to witness this.

12

CASSIAN

*L*ysander is late to meet me in the innermost office, which both of us pretend to share but neither one will ever sit in for long. It used to be my father's, and too much of him lingers here for it to be comfortable. He had a bank of monitors installed behind the desk with views of the nine security cameras. We call it the den. It's not a fucking den.

Two of the unblinking eyes watch the entrances of the building, front and back, but the rest peer endlessly into the two rooms that are the beating heart of our business: the cell and the room. I don't look at either. If I see her now...

If I see her now, I don't know what I'll do.

My brother enters on the tail end of the call he was so desperate to take. "—acceptable." A pause. "No. Tomorrow." Then he hangs up the call, shaking his head from side to side as if it was an interruption and not something he'd scheduled in advance. He slips the phone into his pocket and crosses his arms over his chest. "What is it you wanted, Cassian?"

I could kill him, but I don't. I speak calmly but I'm all business. "Who ordered the contract?"

His eyes flick down to the floor.

"Don't waste another second of my time. Who ordered the contract?"

"It was paid for from the—"

"I *know* who paid for it. I read the file. Who *ordered* the contract?" I keep my hands from balling into fists, but it's a near thing. Every muscle in my body is tensed, waiting, as if she's pulling me back toward her. And why? *Why?* Two days ago, I didn't know she existed. "Who, Lysander? Did someone approach you on the street with a briefcase full of money? Were you drugged in a club and woke up with a signed contract? *Who was it?*"

He's working too damn hard not to meet my eyes, looking over my shoulder at the bank of monitors behind me. "I don't know."

"You don't *know*?" My blood courses hot, scorching like lava, don't touch it or you'll die. *I* might die. "It's one thing to fuck up with the form. It's another to be...completely negligent." How could he not know? He *does* know our protocols. I made sure of that. Is this all to fuck with me?

"You obviously don't know how far you've slipped below standards."

The corner of his mouth twitches and I shift my weight, ready to launch myself across the den and take him down to the floor.

"I don't think *she* knows that, either." It's a dry joke, but the weight in his voice makes me spin around.

There's nothing on either one of the entrance cams, just as I suspected. Nobody approaches this house without good reason. And all's quiet in the room. *I'm* not in there, after all, and it's already been cleaned.

But in the cell...

My blood freezes into ice and fractures into infinite pieces, then rushes back together, hotly, pounding. I almost collapse from the sight on the screen. As quickly as it froze, that same blood pulsates hotly, beating a painful path through my veins.

Because Justice is on her bed.

And she's not sleeping.

Lysander makes a choked noise behind me, somewhere south of a laugh, and I taste it as bitterly as if it happened in my own mouth. Despite the release I just pulled in the shower, I'm instantly, painfully hard at the sight of her, knees spread wide on the bed, her hand positioned between her legs—

I turn to go so quickly that Lysander doesn't have time to

get out of the way. Our shoulders connect as I shove past him.

"That's the spirit," he calls after me. "Show her what—" His voice fades behind the rush of blood pounding mercilessly in my ears. *Show her.* Show her. There's nothing I can show her. She had to know we'd be watching. Nobody in that room has ever assumed they had privacy before. Or maybe she doesn't care. I don't know what infuriates me more. I don't know which makes me want her more.

I'm blinded by the image on the screen, storming through the halls in a cloud tinged red with rage. Some part of me whispers that it's not rage, it's not rage at all, but I can't entertain that voice.

Justice Danes, her hand stroking her legs...

Not without consequence.

At the door to the cell, I punch in the code with stiff fingers and stab another button so that as the door opens she's bathed in a harsh light.

I take one step into the room and breathe in the scent of her arousal. It's saturating the air, taking up all the space in the room, but her hand isn't between her legs anymore. I half hoped she would still be in that obscene position when I entered, just so I could take advantage of it for her punishment, but Justice has had enough time to sit up, panting, naked beneath the thin scrap of a sheet she's pulled from the top of the bed. It half covers her, one peaked nipple exposed, the upper part of her back pressed defensively against the wall.

Her sweet mouth opens and closes. "What are you—" she gasps. "Have you been *watching* me?"

I could nearly laugh at her indignation—very nearly. It's so fucking naive for a woman who spit at me, so innocent, so pure. "Every moment," I growl. "Did you think you had *privacy* in here?" The last word comes out on a sneer and her eyes flick downward. Is that heat on her cheeks? Can she possibly feel shame for what she's done, what she's been caught doing?

But then her eyes meet mine again and I see it's not only shame. It's defiance. That chin comes up a fraction of an inch.

"How dare you." My voice is low, and the question I'm asking has taken on a new shape, a new form. How dare she be so impudent? And how dare she do that, on the bed, without *my* permission, in *my* house, under a fucking contract, no less—

The corners of her mouth turn down with a little frown that does nothing to temper the fire in her eyes. "You never said." She sounds like nothing so much as a petulant student, and it sends another rush of blood straight between my legs.

"I never said," I repeat back, not taking my eyes from hers. I want her to feel this, feel every moment of it.

"You didn't."

"I never said that you could get yourself off while you're here for punishment." How could she believe it would have been all right? Who the hell is this woman?

She bites her lip, drawing it between her white teeth. "If it's so wrong, then punish me."

It's a dare and a crossroads, planted firmly between us. I'm still sorting out what it means that Justice gets off on the punishments I dispense. I'm not a fucking idiot—I know this is a game people play. But *I* am not playing that game. This is a cold, sharp business, and nothing about it is done for fun. Or for pleasure. That's not what people pay me for, and it's not what they paid my father for, either. They paid for pain. They paid for retribution.

They didn't pay for fingers in the folds of a needy, wet pussy.

And now that she's thrown down that gauntlet, now that she's *topping from the bottom* like this is some scene in a sleazy club covered in velvet and jizz...

I can't do it.

Physically, yes. I could take her by the hair and drag her on her knees to the room, I could strap her down, I could pin her across my lap. I could use any of the various tools at my disposal. But that would be giving in to her.

My brain twists and turns at the bonds she's put on it. It's not fucking right. It's wrong, and while I'm standing in the room with her, I can't see the way out of this situation. It's beyond fucked now.

But neither can I turn and go out the door.

I won't let her win.

Not now, not ever.

So instead I let a slow smile creep over my face. Justice blinks at the sight of it, pressing back into the wall a little more, and I wonder if she's regretting what was surely a flippant offer. Because even if she's rubbing it out with her cheek pressed against the sheet, she must know that there's worse I could do. Worse than the belt. Much, much worse.

I cross the room in two strides and she sucks in a breath. Maybe she was less intimidated when I was standing by the door, but now I'm towering over her, looking down at that exposed nipple, at the lean line of her thigh, with nothing between us but a few inches.

Justice tries to hold on to the sheet when I rip it away, but it slips from her fingers.

God, she's perfection.

I can see the marks from the belt curving around the side of her ass from here, and if we were anywhere else, any other people, I'd lean down and kiss her lips. Taste her. Take her. Ravage her.

But we're not anywhere else.

13

I don't know who he is when he reaches for my neck.

But it doesn't matter whether he's Cassian Locke or *Sir* when his fingers slide over my windpipe, his grip strong enough that I know he could kill me but loose enough that I can still breathe. It's not his hand that's making my breath shallow and rough, though I'm desperate to play it cool.

How can I, when I know they've been watching? God, I am so fucking stupid. How could I *be* so stupid? How could I not know that this place would be filled with cameras, every inch of me on display at any given moment?

Maybe you did know, a voice whispers darkly in the back of my mind. Maybe you did know that he was watching, maybe you wanted him to come here...

His hand tightens on my neck and I snap back into this moment, this utterly mortifying, degrading moment, when it could not get any worse than lying naked on this bed with this man's hand wrapped around my neck like I am his property.

My pussy clenches at the thought and heat trails up around my chin.

His property.

I'm not his property, I am being held here against my will.

And yet, and *yet...*

It was still me with my hand between my legs, filthy, panting. Jesus, and now I've dared him to punish me. My ass still hurts from when I was tied over that bench less than an hour ago. The skin still smarts. I can't see how red it is, but I bet it's an angry pink.

"Spread your legs."

I hadn't noticed the way I'd pinned my knees together until he gives the rough command. There's something about his voice that makes me pull my knees apart without thinking until the moment that I *do* think, and then I clamp them back together.

"Spread your legs, or I'll do it for you." There's enough of a threat curled in the rich liquid of his voice that I only hesitate a moment longer before I draw my knees apart, exposing my center to the air. To him.

I'm still wet.

The air licks between my legs, a cool caress.

"Wider."

I have to wriggle down a couple of inches against the wall to allow my legs to open any farther.

"Wider."

Oh, God. This is—this is different. A flush rushes down and across my chest, beginning with his hand and ending between my legs. It's not like being tied by impersonal leather straps. It's not like when he becomes nothing but a shadow dispensing burst after burst of pain.

I spread my legs as wide as they'll go, finally forced to use my hands to press my knees outward. My knees themselves are hinged up awkwardly near my breasts, the gap between them closing with every breath.

His eyes are on mine, like he takes some sick pleasure in watching my face while I follow his orders. A humiliating drip slips from between my legs down to the sheet beneath me. Even over my ragged breathing, I can hear it.

He can, too.

His eyes tear away from mine, alighting on my neck, my breasts. I can almost feel them lingering on my nipples. Damn them. They're giving me away almost as much as the slickness between my legs.

As much as I want to follow his gaze, I can't. Because with the firestorm of his eyes focused somewhere on my face, I can finally look at him. He's got me pinned on my back.

There's nowhere else to look. And I find that I don't want any other view.

Dark hair, not a hint of gray, not a lock out of place. An aquiline nose like something out of a historical movie. He could have been an actor, if he didn't do...this. Punish people. Punish women. Punish *other* women—

A sick flash of jealousy flutters through the pit of my gut. How many other women has he pinned like this, watched like this? And how can I be jealous of them? Were they all dragged here, like me, to pay for their sins?

And did he like it?

I follow the sharp, cutting line of his jaw to his lips. What would it be like to have those lips on mine? To have them *anywhere* on my body? Is he the kind of man who would bite at my nipples? A ripple of pleasure spreads outward from them at the thought of being bitten. Not by any man, by this man, whose power vibrates in every one of his muscles. The cut of his suit doesn't disguise it for an instant. It only enhances it.

He's staring between my legs.

Straight between my legs, where more wetness is gathering like I'm some kind of slut for pain, like I'm some kind of glutton for punishment.

And I am. That's what I am.

I asked him to punish me, and he's doing it now. I am half

consumed by the shame of his hand around my neck and half drowning for the love of it.

I wish we could have met somewhere else. Somewhere we would have been on equal footing. Where he could have seen me as something other than a body to be punished.

You deserve this, that voice whispers, and I know it's right. I deserve every moment of his punishment, and I deserve what I'll get when he sends me back. My heart thuds against my chest, my stomach twisting. And he *will* send me back, because I would deserve that, too. That's what it means to pay the price.

"Pay attention."

His voice cuts through that useless worry, pointless when he has me in his hand like a bird he could crush at any moment. His eyes are on mine again, dark and searching. Hard, like stone. The corner of his mouth twitches upward in some kind of satisfaction. The punishment isn't over, of course it's not, of course he would never be so simple about it.

"Now finish."

Finish. The word rings in my head, my pussy reacting before the meaning fully reaches my brain. I swallow, feeling the curve of his hand pressing against my neck. "Finish?"

"Put those fingers back where they were when I *inter-*

rupted you." He delivers each word with thudding precision.

It should be easy. My hand is already splayed on the bed, my fingers still damp, but with his eyes on mine I am flooded with the kind of embarrassment I never thought I'd feel again. Not since the moment he put me over his lap the very first time.

"Hesitate one more moment and you'll pay for it." His tone is light, but I don't know how much more of this I can take without passing out. The ugly truth, the ugly, terrible truth, is that the more I breathe him in, the more his very breath brushes against my lips, the more I want him.

And I will never deserve him.

I want to fight him.

I want to obey him.

But I have no more time to think about it, because his grip around my neck tightens again and I instinctively gasp in a breath.

"Hand. Between. Your. Legs."

This time I do move, putting my hand back where it was, my middle two fingers centered squarely on my clit. That's where they were when the light turned on, when that door opened, and when I flung myself to the wall like I'd been caught stealing something.

Which, in Cassian Locke's view, I was.

"Finish."

I want air, I need more air, and so I circle my fingers around my clit. Oh, how am I going to—how am I going to come like this, with his hand like that, with his eyes, and his body—

Shame burns through me again, like another wave of a forest fire, because there it is, under my working fingers. Pleasure. Suddenly his hand on my neck is not pressing down, I'm pressing myself into it as if I can't get enough of his touch. I can't get enough of his touch, but I have to settle for my own.

A low moan escapes my lips as I slip my fingers lower, toward where I want him the most, and then, like the filthy slut that I am, I bring my other hand into play, slipping two fingers inside me while I play with my clit. I'm swollen and oversensitive, but I have no choice, I have no choice but to give myself over to this—

"Keep your eyes open."

He's going to see everything, and here I am on the edge with my hands working between my legs, fucking myself, playing with myself, and when I look up into Cassian's eyes, I see something extraordinary happen.

The stone facade slips away, revealing a color in his cheeks, revealing a heated depth in his eyes, and when he swallows hard, I know—I *know*—he wants me. He wants this.

And I don't have time to think about what that means

because even imagining him wanting me is enough to send me twisting in his grip, coming with a mewling cry that I don't recognize, pleasure bursting through every inch of me. I've ruined the sheets, I had to have, and as the last wave moves over me, my muscles go limp and loose.

He's inches from my face and I reach for him.

God help me, I reach for him, and he leans closer, so close his breath is hot on my chin, and for a wild moment I think he really might kiss me and I am sucked into a vortex of anticipation that I never want to leave, because what happens after we kiss, oh God, it could be, it could *be*—

He releases me.

I hit the bed with a muffled *thud*.

He turns on his heel and stalks out.

14

*A*ll the sun in the world couldn't burn away the shame that's settled over my skin like a fine film, but the sun doesn't know that. The light is weak midmorning in the fall. Weak and pathetic. Lukewarm. Like my self-control.

I almost kissed her tonight.

With her pulse under my fingertips, I was on top of the world. That little neck, so delicate, framed by the loose locks of her hair fallen from the twist they'd put it in that morning. Justice might be a spitfire, but she's flesh and bone like every other woman I've taken under my hand. I've had my fingers wrapped around plenty of necks, but none like hers. None in the cell.

I've never once gone into the cells for one of the contracts.

Why would I?

None of them have interested me outside of the check they come attached to. I don't concern myself with the various webs spun between New York's elite. They shift so much that the information may as well be meaningless. What matters is that I have always been impartial. My *father* has always been impartial. We carefully consider the information on the contract, then approve or decline. There are no feelings involved.

There *were* no feelings involved.

I take a right turn onto Seventh Avenue. My father would have called it prudent to take a car, but I had to get out. Finding Franklin Keys is the perfect excuse.

Mr. Keys is the only person I could find who is publicly associated with the Danes Family Trust. I grit my teeth at the thought of my careless idiot of a brother agreeing to this contract in the first place, and take a deep inhale of the autumn air. The watery sunlight is tinged with a faint edge of chill, still far-off enough that the rest of the city seems to be ignoring it.

I, for one, am going to pay attention.

Mr. Keys' office is another three blocks down in a narrow building wedged between two others. He shares it with one other company—K.L.M., Inc.—and that name means nothing to me. A buzzer by the handle of the glass door summons a doorman, who takes one look at me and presses a switch on the inside. The lock clicks inside the door and the doorman pulls it open.

"Good morning." He nods his head and steps back to let me in. "Do you have an appointment, sir?"

"I'm an old friend of Franklin's." I don't give him the hint of a smile, and he doesn't give me one, either.

We consider each other.

"He'll be expecting me."

The doorman must conclude correctly that today is not a good day to fuck with me. He gives another nod and steps back behind a small podium, ridiculously sized even for the narrow room. It's not even large enough to cover the lower half of his body. He picks up a phone, murmurs something into it, and looks back up at me. "You can go up."

There are two doors at the back of the lobby, each with a brass nameplate. Mr. Keys' is on the left. The knob turns smoothly under my hand, and I open it to find a staircase carpeted in faded green. Ten steps up, and I'm on another landing.

A woman in a navy suit sits behind a wooden desk that's the same shade as the doorframe behind her chair. She stands without a word and opens the door, keeping her eyes on the floor. It occurs to me that these people think I'm someone else.

Fine with me.

I go into Franklin Keys' office and find him cowering behind a desk that's far too large for the room.

No. He's not cowering, exactly, but when he stands up to shake my hand, there's a wobble in the movement that makes me think he could be blown over by a strong gust of wind despite how stocky he is. His hair is dyed a jet black that doesn't suit his face and combed back from a part straight out of the forties.

"How can I help you?" He sits back down with a huff of breath and folds his hands on the surface of his desk. His eyes are a pale imitation of the color blue. Justice's put his to shame.

I shake her out of my thoughts. "I'm here about the Danes Family Trust."

Some of the tension releases from his shoulders. "I can't talk about that." He moves as if to stand up, so I step around the chair opposite his and sit down, leaning back as if I own this entire building and the block surrounding it.

I lean forward into the silence, letting him see my face. I'm trying my best to broadcast an expression that's more thoughtful than menacing, but from the looks of Franklin Keys, I'm failing. And I only half care. "There are questions that need answers, Mr. Keys."

He exhales through his nose and releases his hands, laying them flat on the table between us. "I'm afraid there's nothing I can say about the...trust...you've mentioned."

"The problem is..." I wrinkle my forehead. "I've received

quite a large payment from that trust. A payment for services that are in the process of being rendered. And I've come to question whether that payment was legitimate."

He raises his eyes from the surface of the table. "Did the funds not...transfer properly?"

"Oh, no. They transferred straight into my accounts. But I'm not entirely certain that the Danes family authorized the payment."

"What—" Keys swallows hard. "What reason do you have to believe that?"

"The request for services was unusual."

He waits. Maybe he thinks I'm going to provide more details, but I'm not. I don't divulge the nature of my business to people like Franklin Keys. The individuals who need my services already know who I am, and the individuals who will be on the receiving end will find out when they need to know.

I cock my head to the side. "Did you approve the transfer yourself? You're the trust administrator. It appears on all the available paperwork."

This is the moment that Franklin Keys should throw me out of his office and refuse to provide any kind of confidential information about transfers or anything else. He should never have admitted to being the Franklin Keys involved with the Danes Family Trust in the first place. But he's sweating and clearly scared, and he's not that kind of man.

"What was your name, Mr...?"

"Locke. The payment would have been to Locke Confidential."

I half expect him to pull out a paper record book, but Keys doesn't so much as glance toward any of the drawers. "Yes. I approved that payment." The look in his eyes tells me that he did, in fact, approve the payment.

I watch him for another moment to see if some evidence of a lie crosses his face, but it doesn't. "One more question, Mr. Keys. Which of the Danes directed you to make the payment in the first place?"

He shoves himself up out of his seat. "I have an appointment. I'm afraid I'll need you to leave the office." Franklin Keys is not taller than I am, but he is significantly wider, and the fact of him squeezing around the desk prompts me to stand up and head for the door. I draw a card from my jacket pocket and slap it down on his desk.

"If you remember who gave you the direction to transfer the funds, I'll be available here."

He's practically hyperventilating as he opens the door and stands in front of it, looking everywhere around him but at me. "It's an..." I lose the rest of his sentence because he mumbles it under his breath.

"What was that, Mr. Keys?"

"Fathers and sons." He straightens up as tall as he can.

"Surely, you understand, Mr. Locke. You must understand." He's still mumbling something about understanding when I step out onto the stairs and the door closes quickly behind me.

Fathers and sons.

But Justice is a daughter.

15

JUSTICE

I struggle against the bonds, jerking my wrists from side to side. I've been here for what seems like forever. Maybe longer than forever. At least since sometime this morning, but I have no idea what time it is now. There are no clocks in the punishment room. Cassian must like his sessions to feel endless, and this one already is, even though it hasn't started yet.

Or maybe it has. Mika woke me roughly this morning. The fact that she could surprise me at all was a disappointment, but at some point last night I fell into a deep sleep. But not dreamless. No. Not dreamless at all.

I woke up with my thighs pressed together, the space between them hot and wet, and she frowned at me as if I'd done something wrong. But Cassian wouldn't have told her about that, would he? No. Because it came so close to turning into something else entirely.

I can't talk about the ways they cleaned me up this morning. I'd thought being forced to have a wax was over the line. Now I know it's not.

I'm in the middle of considering whether he's making me wait like this because he's still upset about last night when the door flings open and Cassian strides in. I catch a glimpse of him out of the corner of my eye but then he's gone. I don't dare turn my head to watch him. It's possible I *do* dare, but after how intimate his idea of a punishment was last night, I'm going to think twice before challenging him again.

So I remain silent, hotly aware of the way this position exposes me to him in a way that's almost as demeaning as the way I was spread out for him last night. At least he can't see the way my nipples stand erect if he's standing directly behind me.

No...actually, he probably can.

He's shifting around behind me. There's a rustle of fabric —taking off his jacket, rolling up his sleeves—and enduring the wait is agony. Is his palm going to land across my ass without warning? Is he going to start counting? Is he going to mention what happened last night?

Does he still want me?

I rock back against the bonds a fraction of an inch, just enough to release some of the tension building between my shoulder blades. It's not altogether uncomfortable to be bent over like this, on display like this, but it's not altogether comfortable, either.

"I hate liars."

Cassian speaks the words as if he's relaying the weather forecast. It's so casual that it lands sharply on my ears, and I open my mouth to reply, leaving it open for a long moment before snapping my lips shut.

He hasn't asked me a question, and now I'm trembling in anticipation. I don't know if it's pleasurable anticipation or unadulterated fear. It's both, one landing after the other, trading places like a couple twirling around a dance floor.

"You're a liar."

So there's the follow-up.

"I—"

"Keep that pretty little mouth of yours closed. You'll have enough reason to open it shortly."

He steps closer and the air in the room responds to his body, whispering across my naked ass. "I don't like liars, and pretending not to know something is the same as lying. It's incredible that I'd have to tell a woman like you a simple fact like that, but clearly, I do."

My body lights up with shame, from the top of my head to the tip of my toes. That heat is followed by an icy cold dash of something else—guilt or fear or all of it at once.

He knows, that dark voice whispers. *He knows what you've done. He knows you're as guilty as sin.*

I want to tell him that I'm not. I want to tell him that I've tried my best not to be guilty, even while I live the life that was offered to me. I can't help it that I was born to the parents that I was, I can't help it that they built the empire they did, I can't—

His hand slams down hard on my left ass cheek, and the pain chases the shame into the back corner of my mind.

It surprises me enough to draw a little noise out of my mouth, but I press my lips tightly together.

Another blow, to the other ass cheek.

"You can admit what you've done." Cassian's voice cuts like a razor and his hand might as well be a belt. It feels like he's barely holding back, but he must be. He must be holding back something.

Slap. Slap. Slap.

He settles into a rhythm, and how many has he delivered before I'm making noise? Ten? Twenty?

It's somewhere after twenty that I lose count.

But it's long before twenty that I'm wet.

"You'll still receive the punishment you deserve." He's so cool, so matter-of-fact about it. "But you can admit it. Confession is good for the soul."

I can't confess. I cannot. That is the one thing I cannot do, and I know it as certainly as I know that this is going to be a long, hard session. This one will leave a mark. Still, it doesn't matter. Confession might be good for the soul, but it is bad for the body. It's lethal for the body.

My family is lethal.

That's the only thought I allow to cross my mind, the only thought that can break through the heat blooming across my ass, the deep, aching pain that makes me...

...hot.

Hot for him.

Hot for *this*.

So hot that even when he stops, I don't stop moving. I can't. I can barely move an inch, I'm so tightly restrained, but I rock my hips as much as I can. God, if only I could make contact with the bench, if only I could...

I so want his hand between my legs.

I receive the harsh pelting of a belt across my thighs instead. It's a bright-white leather pain, and the first blow makes me scream. I know, intellectually, somewhere in the part of my mind that's still processing regular thoughts, that it could get worse, but it's the accumulation of all the sensations that tears the cry from my mouth.

"I hate liars, but I love that sound."

Cassian's words ring like a bell just before the next stripe

lands. The two things together—the words and the belt
—are a shock. In that instant, something clarifies in my
mind. This isn't about me.

This is *not* about me.

Cassian has never said anything about himself before a
punishment. It has always been a transaction, and the
transaction is not between us. It's between him and
someone else, and I'm only caught in the middle. But he
loves the sound of my scream so I let out another one. A
tear slips from the corner of my eye. The belt trips against
something—the side of his leg?—and then he is a
shadow next to my head.

He presses a thumb to my cheek where the tear has
fallen, and I turn just enough to see what he's doing. He
lifts that hand to his mouth, and then he licks the salt on
his skin.

From me.

It takes my breath away.

"Confess."

At first I can't speak. He's knocked all the air out of me
and then some. But I force an inhalation of breath into
my lungs. "You're—no—priest."

That flame lights behind his dark eyes, behind the eyes of
the man who has tasted my tears, and I see in his face
that he wants more of them.

But *I* want more of them, too.

Not tears.

The pain.

Because it feels like something else. Something else is twisted up in it that makes me feel so alive.

So absolved.

That's not what Cassian came here to do, but he's doing it anyway, and I can't explain it—I can't explain anything. I can only wait as he moves back around behind me.

There's a ringing silence, a silence as cold and delicate as the first snow in winter, and then the belt lands against me again in a red fury. Once. Twice. Three times. Then he adjusts the angle and wraps it around to my inner thighs, soft flesh that's only been touched by grasping hands and my own fingertips. All I can think about is getting my clit to the surface of the bench. All I can think about is how filthy this makes me, how shameful...

How much I want it.

If he would just reach between my legs and give me release, I would be his forever.

You are already his forever.

The voice blends in with Cassian's. He's saying something, but I only catch "—for the paddle."

I'm shuddering, shaking on the bench, but he moves to the front of me, to the wall where the tools hang, and I blink through hazed eyes as he selects one and returns to his previous position behind me.

"Four strokes." His voice shines with authority. With power. I'm tied down. He loves it. I love it. I— "And then I'll decide how many more."

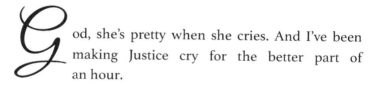od, she's pretty when she cries. And I've been making Justice cry for the better part of an hour.

I'm very nearly finished.

"Last one," I say into the sound of her breathing, each inhale a gasp, each exhale ragged.

I've gone too far, and I know it.

I've lost all sense of the boundaries I normally clutch to with white-knuckled fists. We are outside the contract now. No contract I've ever accepted has called for punishments this sustained. Some of them have been close—some of them have been maddeningly specific in the pain they want to inflict—but I have to admit that this stopped being about administering an agreement a long time ago. Before I even stepped into the room.

The cane balances so perfectly in my hand. It's rattan, varnished, with a little bit of give—a vicious thing. And it hardly ever enters the picture with contracts. They can only handle so much, and I prefer to stretch it out, to make it last, to make an *impact*.

It's made an impact on Justice. The three stripes across her red ass are angrier by far than anything else I've done to her.

I should stop.

But I don't want to.

I want more.

My blood sings with it, rages with it, even as she shivers against the straps of the bench. Her breath huffs out in little cries that sound on the verge of begging. I'm not sure she knows she's making any noise, and I don't care.

One more. One more.

I bring the cane back and let it fly through the air with a whistle as sharp as a knife. When it lands, it sends her head jerking forward, her entire body tensing and pulling, but there's nowhere to go. I have expertly restrained her. Of course I have. And the cry that tears from her throat is raw. It echoes in my ears. It runs down into my blood and through every one of my veins, a silvery, sick pleasure.

This is different.

I walk to the wall with its hangers lined up for every

implement and put the cane back into its place, the rushing in my head so loud it blocks out every other sound, even Justice's fresh wave of sobs.

In an instant, the knowledge screeches to a halt at the center of me.

I've gone too far.

I knew that before the last stroke, but now I know it in a different way. Down to the marrow in my bones, I know it, and I press a fist to my lips to keep in the noise that threatens to come loose.

It felt so good.

It felt so fucking good.

And why? Because she defied me? Because she spit at my feet the first time she saw me? Because she resisted, and resisted, and because I loved the look of her spread out underneath me far more than I've loved any other sight in my wretched life? Did I think I could punish that out of my own head by punishing her? Did I think I could erase the tangled knots of this contract, the twisting stupidity of my own brother, by destroying the white flesh of her bottom?

It's an awful pleasure that throbs through me now. I liked it, everything I did to her. I wanted it. I craved it. I have craved it from the moment my father let me take over a contract.

I can't think.

I turn back toward her and I should feel guilty at the sight of her, hanging uselessly in her restraints, bent over the bench that humiliates all of them. Not a single contract has been able to hold in her tears across the bench, but I've never drawn so many from one woman.

Mika's shadow hovers outside the door. I can see where her feet break up the light from the hallway in the slim crack at the bottom of the doorframe, waiting. According to protocol, I should walk out of here right now and let my assistant come in to clean up the mess. It's Mika who should release the restraints one by one, then clip Justice's hands into cuffs and lead her back to her cell. That is the nature of the punishment. Pain, and then solitude.

But I can't move.

I drink her in.

The curve of her ass, still on display, still ready for punishment. The slim nip of her waist. Her breasts, pressed against the bench. She held herself up at the beginning of the punishment, as much as she could. It gave her an inch or so of clearance. Now she slumps against the leather, her cheek pressed to the smooth surface, eyes squeezed shut.

Tears falling, falling.

As they should. The stripes on her ass are only the topmost layer of the pain I caused. With my hand. With the belt. With the paddle. Thinking of it sends another surge of blood to my cock. I didn't think I could get any harder. It turns out I can.

Justice opens her eyes.

The blue is heightened, magnified, by the red, puffy skin of her eyelids and her pink cheeks. I've been cruel. I worked the belt over the insides of her thighs, but I came back to the flesh of her ass again and again. I could've spread it out over the rest of her body, but I didn't, I let all the pain center there. But I can see in her eyes that it didn't stay put.

It never does, does it?

At first, her gaze is somewhere in the middle distance, as if she doesn't notice that I'm there at all.

But then she lifts her eyelashes and looks straight at me.

The look in her eyes stops my heart.

Because it's not a look that sings of betrayal, of a crushed soul, of a broken girl. I've seen enough of those expressions to know when it's happened.

It's a look that's pure need.

Her lips part, the pink skin shining from the tears that have fallen over her face, and my heart seizes. I know what she's going to say. It'll be a curse. She'll be raging against what I've done to her, desperate to get back to her cell and...

"Please."

It's a broken word, split down the middle by a sob, and at first it doesn't make any sense.

And then it does.

"Please." Her voice is a little louder this time, but no less ragged.

My entire soul bends toward her, but I don't move an inch. Instead, I steel myself for what has to come next. She can beg all she wants, but I won't free her. Not for another three days. Five full days, that's what the contract says, and that's what I'll stick to.

I remember myself, what I'm supposed to be doing, and I take a step toward the door.

"No," she cries. "Please don't go."

It freezes me in place.

"Sir." The word sends a shiver down my spine that threatens to wrack my entire body. "Please...*please.*"

Nothing in the world should keep me in this room at this moment, but those words out of her mouth command my attention. I drag my eyes back to hers and search for the words to answer her. It's the wrong idea, it's absolutely wrong, but I'm going to answer. Her plea is a hook dug right into the center of my chest. "Why would you want me to stay?"

My tone is acid—even I can hear that—but she doesn't flinch. No. That little movement is her hips, rising and falling, and for the first time I allow myself to see her.

To see all of her.

That tiny rock of her hips is a dead giveaway. Her face floods with fresh color, a shame that I can't help but delight in.

"Please. I—I need you."

I need you.

They fall like a boulder onto ice, shattering everything beneath it. *Need you.* Who has ever needed me to do anything in this room other than leave? I have felt it coming off each contract in waves.

I move behind her as if drawn there by a puppet master. And there, between Justice's legs, is all the evidence I need that she is telling the truth.

Her pussy, despite having been absolutely untouched for the entirety of our session, is swollen and pink and dripping. She can't close her thighs against me, and it seems she doesn't want to, because even though she's tied down to the bench, it's like she feels my gaze and tries to spread her legs a little wider.

Her body begs for me to touch her.

"Oh, God," Justice sobs, and it hits me all at once that she is not crying because I've pushed her past the point of unbearable pain. Her need for release is what's unbearable.

I'm moving closer before I realize what I'm doing, before I

can stop myself, and I reach out and put one hand on the small of her back.

A brand new sob, of a different tenor, rips from her throat, and I can feel her pressing back into my touch.

"Lower, oh, please, lower, oh—"

She is begging me to slip my fingers down over her surely throbbing ass and into the most intimate parts of her. My cock twitches against my pants.

"Sir, please—"

I jerk my hand away like her skin is a hot stove.

Justice howls, and then she's babbling *no, no, no, please, no.*

"Silence." It's almost a shout, a last desperate attempt to stop this runaway train.

I throw myself through the door so fast I almost tackle Mika to the floor.

"Mr. Locke? Should I—Mr. Locke? Mr. Locke?"

"Yes." I bite the word over my shoulder. Her footsteps go quickly toward the cell.

I'm blind, a mess, lurching down the hallway like a drunk, and I don't look back.

17

*E*ach minute in my rooms is a razor dragging its blade across my skin. It's slow, such an agonizingly slow pain, and nothing I do will relieve it.

I want her.

I want her here with *me*.

I want her to be mine.

Mine.

And not mine in a temporary way, the way all the contracts belong to me for the length of their punishment —a *permanent* way.

It's impossible.

I tighten my hands into deliberate fists and release them, settling back into a chair in front of my fireplace. From a perch on the corner table my mother watches me from the stillness of a picture frame.

It's the only one left in the house.

The photograph was taken at least a decade ago on a vacation to the south of France. She's standing in the surf, holding her hat on her head with one hand. She could be anyone's mother, beautiful even in middle age, but her face is enough like mine that I couldn't deny her even if I wanted to.

I don't want to.

And I don't want to betray her.

The truth is a ticking vessel in the corner of my brain. I locked it there when I sent her away. My father was newly dead of an alleged heart attack, somewhere in the bowels of a Family compound overseas, and I saw the writing on the wall before the call came in.

It had been one indiscretion, on my father's part from what I understand, though the details have always been vague. There was a contract he shouldn't have taken. There was undisclosed involvement with the Family and it had ended with a summons to Europe. The summons had concluded with him in a casket.

My mother was smuggled out of the States the same day we got the news. The next day—

I stand up from the chair and pace in front of the fire.

The next day it was made clear that all of this would become my responsibility.

Rich families don't want their business aired in court. Neither does the Family.

Absolute discretion has always been the standard.

And here I am, fighting against the bonds of those standards like a contract bent over my bench.

She's not dead, the truth whispers, and I shove it back into its place. If I don't let it in, it won't be so hard.

It's one contract. One woman. Behind closed doors. There is nothing to indicate that allowing myself one pleasure would have the kind of effect—

Somehow I've arrived at the door to my rooms and I slam the side of my fist into its panel. There is *every* indication that a single pleasure could bring everything crumbling to the ground.

And yet.

Yet.

There's a knock at the door. "Mr. Locke?"

It's Mika's soft voice. I don't know if she's been lurking outside or if the sound carried far enough for my staff to hear.

"Everything's fine." I force the words through gritted teeth and wait for her footsteps to retreat.

They do.

A need like this could eat a man alive. In Justice's eyes, I've already seen flashes of the future without her. A version of myself gaunt and pale and wasted. I need to drink her rage and her pleasure and her pain like I need water. A man can survive without food for far longer. I'd survive without food forever if it meant one night with her.

I go back to the table with the photograph and pick up the frame in my hands. My mother smiles out at me. It's like she knows.

Even Lysander doesn't know. Not the truth about Justice...and not the truth about our mother.

Given his recent behavior, he can *never* know.

"I'm sorry." The whispered apology falls only on the frame of the photograph, the anguish that cracks my voice heard by no one. It'll never reach her ears, if I do my job.

And I *will* do it.

I will do it every day until I'm released from its strictures.

But tonight, I'm taking her for my own.

18

*S*ilence.

Silence drips into the cell like rain, like that water torture I've read about on the internet.

There was no sound as that woman bound my wrists and led me back to my cage like a dog. She motioned for me to lay on the bed, and I did, my face pressed into the pillow. There was nothing to say, so I said nothing when she left the room and came back a minute or two later. I kept my eyes closed when she stepped up next to the bed, and after a pause felt gentle hands on the smarting skin of my ass. It soothed, wherever she touched. Not much. Enough so I could stand it.

I don't dare turn over, still.

He caned me.

He *caned* me, and I lay over that bench with my pussy throbbing.

Why am I like this? What has made me so desperate, so depraved, that the only thing in the world that I want is Cassian Locke's hand between my legs? Why do I want the kind of relief only he can give me? Why?

Because he's the first person to see your sins and wash them clean.

The thought comes unbidden, and I don't understand it. I only believe in sins in the abstract. I knew there was nothing holy about the world from a young age. You can't grow up in my father's house without knowing that. But here I am, with the word *sins* ringing in my ears and throbbing between my legs.

I don't press my thighs together because they're bruised. He belted me there, too, and like some kind of hungry slut, I sank into that pain like a fucking lover's caress.

But there was never any relief. No. That's not what I'm here for. I'm here for punishment.

I don't know why I'm here. I assume it's because of what I did, but I don't know who would have wanted me to pay.

Not specifically. Not...with a name. Or a face.

I gather the energy to turn over onto my side, being careful not to roll too far onto my ass, and another tear slips onto my cheek. God, with the crying. Too much punishment can break a person, everyone knows that.

But I don't feel broken by the punishment. I feel broken by that one, glancing touch. His fingers on my back. He was so close. He was *so* close, I could feel it, and then he ran out of the room like he discovered I was a sorceress.

I need him, still.

Even now.

I push myself up onto my elbow, trying to get more air into my lungs, and the door to my cell flies open.

It startles me. The past two days I've tried not to show any kind of surprise when these things happen, but my nerves are stretched tightly and I let out a gasp, scrambling to sit up. That's a mistake. My ass is *sore,* oh, God, the pain is so fresh. He left marks.

I want more marks.

I roll onto my hip before I see who's standing in the middle of the cell.

"Sir?"

"Don't call me that now." I don't recognize his voice, it's so different from the way he sounds when we're in that room. It's different even from the way he sounded last night, when he pinned me to this bed by my throat.

"I need to," I whisper.

He comes closer, dropping to his knees in front of me. It's so unlike him that I rear back. Has he decided to kill me? Is he going to ask forgiveness first?

"You don't know what you need from me." His hand comes out and he braces himself against the bed. "You don't know me at all. You have no idea what I'm capable of."

"I do." My voice is still shaking, but I wish it was strong. "I know. And I want it."

"Get up."

He stands, and my brain struggles to catch up. "What?"

"Get up. You're coming with me."

I don't know how I get up from the bed. He doesn't help me, and my legs wobble underneath me. Cassian strides for the door and stops, silhouetted in the light from the hallway.

"Where are you taking me?"

I can't see his face, and he doesn't answer, only steps into the hall.

I follow him.

It's deserted here, like I thought it would be, but he turns the opposite direction—away from the room where he punishes me. No, that's not right. He can punish me in any room. My chest goes tight. Maybe there's another room, a *worse* room, where he's taking me now to....do what? What could he do to me that's worse than what he's already done?

And then there's that voice, a seductive whisper. *What could he do that's better?*

There's another door at the end of the hall, one with a touchpad next to the frame, and Cassian raises a hand and punches in a long code like he's been doing it all his life. Probably he has. The door slides open, and he steps through the opening.

"Are you coming?" The lines of his face are sharp in the light, even though the hallway where he's standing is...different.

The carpet where I'm standing is white, with enough plush pile that my bare feet sink into it a bit. But there's a clear demarcation between where I'm standing and where he's standing. There's an intricate pattern under his feet that blends with the color of the trim. My part of the hallway has trim that's the same blue as the walls. It's purposeful, meant to divide us. A tremble moves through my hips when I think about crossing that line, and until two days ago, I never would have given it a moment's consideration.

"Let me rephrase that." The tenor of his voice changes so that it resembles the *sir* I've known for the past two days. "Come here."

I'm still ashamed at how fast my body responds to *that*. A drip of wetness slides down the inside of my thigh, the air evaporating it in a burst of cool.

One step over the line and I'm by his side.

Naked.

I am always naked in my cell. I am always naked in the punishment room. But here? Where *is* here? I'm aware of it with a cascade of prickles all over my exposed skin. For all I know, any of the doorways in this hallway could open, and anyone could come out, and then—

Then what?

I'm here to be punished. That's what I know about...all of this. I know I was hauled off the streets and brought here. I fought. I know that. It was me that fought them. My stomach lurches. I thought being returned to my family was the worst possible outcome, but it's not, is it? The worst possible outcome is to be...

I can hardly dare to think the word.

Sold.

Cassian's eyes are on me—I can feel them—for another burning moment and then he turns and moves down the hallway. I hurry to keep up with him. Every step reminds me of what he's done with a kind of stretching pain across my ass, but my mind whirls with the new possibilities. Am I the dumbest person on the face of the planet? How could this not have occurred to me before?

He makes one right turn down a narrow hallway where the light is dimmer and I follow him closely, my breath loud in my ears. He raises his hand to another keypad, this time entering a shorter code. This door opens soundlessly and he slips through.

It's...a secret passage.

That's what it has to be.

There is no decoration, and the carpet here is thinner, of lower quality. It scrapes against the soles of my feet as I follow him. The lighting here is only two strips along the lower corners of the walls, so I know this isn't a place meant for public consumption. No one is meant to see this. A thrill of excitement blooms and dies at the pit of my gut. There's no way to know if this is good or bad. No way to know at all.

How many steps is it down the hall? I forget to keep track, but Cassian pauses again. One more doorway. One more touchpad. I crane my neck to look behind us—that other door is closed now. The one in front of us slides open, and Cassian's shoulders drop an inch. Then he stops, holding out his arm like he's ushering me into a party.

"Go in." This is no less a command, and I follow it, preceding him into the room. The door closes with a swish behind us.

It's not *a* room. It's a suite. We've stepped into a kind of den, with an overstuffed sofa facing a roaring fireplace. There are two chairs flanking the sofa, and as we stand there, the lights come up around us.

Smart lights. An expensive touch.

Cassian shifts behind me, and I spin to face him.

The expression he's wearing is like nothing I've ever seen.

"Why am I here?"

The question tumbles out from between my lips before I can stop it. Cassian watches my lips move, his eyes dropping away from mine, and the air between us crackles with an energy I can hardly bear to breathe in. It's like the walls between us have been dropped away.

"Surely you're not so naive."

He has a beautiful voice. It's rich and low, almost like a song.

I swallow before I answer. "I don't think of myself as naive. But that doesn't mean I know why I'm here."

"Be more specific when you speak. It will save time."

He doesn't waste any time, does he?

"I want to know both things. I want to know why I'm in this room, and I want to know why I'm in your...house. I'm assuming this is your house."

"And you think now is the time when we should be honest with each other?"

I shrug one shoulder, feeling my nakedness more with the way my breast lifts and falls. "You brought me here, so...yes."

"The only reason people come to my home through the back entrance is because they're under contract." His eyes are so dark, so fixed on my skin.

"What does that mean?"

He steps forward, closing the distance between us in one step. I watch his hand rise to meet my chin, and at the first touch of his fingertips, grazing the line of my jaw and down to my throat, I let out a moan. "Are you sure you want to know?"

19

CASSIAN

I can't fucking help myself.

Away from those rooms, the distance between us is a taunt, a tease, and I can't say another word without getting closer. So I do. God help me, I do. And that sound she makes when I touch her lights up parts of me I never knew existed.

Being affected like this by a woman was never in the cards for me. How could it be? The business is all that has ever mattered. And being in charge of this business means having as few weaknesses as possible. That's what it means to be an impartial arbiter in the kinds of high-stakes disputes that rich people want to sweep under the rug.

But I am affected.

I can't help it.

"Answer me."

I'm like a moth wending its way toward a flame. I go toward her knowing I'm going to get burned, but I have to do it anyway. At least once. This raw sensation, this wide-open feeling—I can't turn away from it. Not yet. I've never felt it before. Never allowed myself to feel it before.

That was a smart fucking decision, because a man could be brought to his knees this way. And I can't afford to kneel to anyone.

I see the way her body responds when I command her this way. Justice fought like a wildcat, but clearly she's been waiting for submission all her life.

"Yes," she whispers.

This moment feels easier than the others. It's another one in a series of moments where I should make the opposite decision. I know the stakes. I know the business rides on this. But with my hand on her skin, all of it fades into the background.

"A person under contract has been brought to me for punishment. Or, in broader terms, to settle a deal. Or a dispute."

Her eyelashes flutter as she opens her eyes, but she's still, like she's worried the slightest movement will make me release her. "Disputes? For who?"

An alarm bell goes off in the back of my mind, but it's probably an innocent question. It wouldn't be beneath some of my clients to send a woman to get under my skin, to get confidential information, but a woman who had been sent for that purpose would never behave like Justice has behaved.

"For the people who can afford to pay me."

A question flashes through her eyes then. "Who paid you for—for me?"

I run my thumb along the curve of her jaw, and she trembles beneath my touch. She may be trembling, but her nipples are hard little pebbles that I want to run my thumb over.

I resist the urge, but I get more purchase on her jaw with my fingers and tilt her face to mine. Blue eyes, like a summer day in the Mediterranean. An endless blue, like flying. Soaring. "That's a bit of a mystery."

She furrows her brow. "You kidnapped me and you don't know why?"

That makes me laugh, the way she says it, and the sound feels unfamiliar in my mouth. "I didn't kidnap you."

"No." The word is a whisper, almost a sigh. "You have other people to do your dirty work."

It draws another laugh. "I do all the dirty work in this business. And the acquisition of contracts isn't usually such an...ordeal."

She tips her head back another inch, exposing more of her throat to me. She might as well be Polyxena, ready to bleed out in front of Achilles. Only Justice's sacrifice won't end any wars. It might begin a few of them. "People just come here? Of their own free will?"

"I wouldn't bring free will into it. Most of the contracts arrive with some knowledge of what they're paying the price for."

Her lashes lower then, and a deeper shade of blush spreads over her cheekbones. "Then you must know what I'm paying for."

The nearness of her is intoxicating. She's been punished, and all I can smell is the scent of the soap on her skin and something that's purely *her* underneath, like...sunshine. It sounds ridiculous even in my head to think it, but it's true. And then there's the scent of her arousal, which must be leaking between her legs.

"I don't care what anyone's paying for," I growl, and it gets her attention, because those eyes lock on my face again. "I'm never invested in what goes on between families in this city. I'm here to collect a hefty payment when they want something settled, and that's all. It's what my own family is known for. But with you, precious thing—" A full body shiver rocks her at those words. "I can't even muster a passing interest at what you've done or not done. The crimes you've committed or not committed..." I bring my other hand up to cradle the back of her head and stroke my fingers down the side of her neck, tracing the line of her shoulder and then moving around to her collarbone. Her curves send my fingers on a pathway straight to her nipple, and I circle one without touching it directly. The peak rises a little more. "I am...curious about you in other ways." I keep my tone utterly conversational, because it seems to be working wonders on Justice.

"What ways?" Her reply is breathy and light, and I'm not imagining it—she shifts her feet another inch outward, spreading her legs for me even now. So fucking wanton. I love it.

"I want to know why you fought me so hard."

"I—I didn't know—I didn't know why—" The patterns of her speech are broken up by the fact that I'm still tracing around her nipples, one by one, then dipping a finger down toward her navel, but not lower than that. "I didn't know why this was happening."

"But you do know. Because you think someone has a personal vendetta against you. Tell me. What was it? Did you break off an engagement? Cross a man you weren't supposed to? Insult someone during an important business transaction?"

"I—" The word dies out as soon as it crosses her lips, and no more follow. Not that I really care. I do care, in general, but not in this moment.

I lean in close, so my lips nearly brush the shell of her ear. "I want to know what you taste like."

She lets out a moan that's the cousin of a sob, and I pull back to watch the relief dawn on her face like a new sunrise. "What else?"

"I want to know how you feel when you tighten around my cock. I want to be buried in you." Softer, softer, so she has to lean in to listen, so she's hanging on my every word. "I want to know what it's like to fuck you with a punished ass, with my hips driving into that raw flesh with every stroke.

I have been holding back. I have been teasing myself as much as I'm teasing her, because there's nothing I want more than to feel the heat between her legs. But there's one last shred of me that's clinging to the standards my father set for our business years ago. And I know that if I touch her there, I will be lost entirely.

Yet the act of resistance is like resisting the urge to breathe. I allow it to go on for one more draw of air into my lungs, and then I trace the path from the hollow of her neck down between her legs. Justice's hips rock forward, begging, and her hand comes up to cover mine on her neck, pressing it into her skin so that I won't let go.

My fingertips meet heat, meet wetness, meet flesh that's pouting with need, and I break.

I sweep Justice into my arms with one movement, not being careful of the abused flesh of her ass. She lets out a little cry of pain that feels like a jolt of pure oxygen as I carry her across the room to the sofa and deposit her on it in a heap.

"Get up." The commands come so easily to me, and for once, obeying comes easily to her. Justice scrambles to her knees, gripping the back of the sofa for all she's worth. "Spread your legs. Wider. Press your ass out, toward me."

She does, making a sound in the back of her throat that's half invitation, half warning.

I bring my hand down on the stripes across her ass fast. Hard. Without warning.

Justice lets out a strangled cry, but she spreads her legs another inch wider.

"You're a slut for the pain, aren't you?" It's a rhetorical question, but her head drops forward. It almost looks like a nod. And she does not move her ass an inch. She doesn't cower, doesn't flinch.

"Tell me how ashamed you are."

"I'm *so* ashamed." Her voice is filled with tears and it lights a fire up every inch of my spine. "I should—I should be fighting you. I should have kept fighting you every moment, no matter what—no matter what you did. But—" A real sob rips from her throat.

"But you needed that pain."

I give her another strike across the ass, the pulse pounding in my ears. I should *not* be doing this. There is no way I should punish her even another stroke.

"I...deserve it," she chokes out. "I was pretending I didn't, I was trying to believe I didn't, but I—I deserve it."

What could make her deserve this? It's for my own pleasure that I'm being so harsh, and my hand aches to spank her again. Justice is shaking, close to the edge. And I want to know. I want to know what secret she's keeping, what awful, dark thing she's submitting to punishment for. Because we're beyond the contract, and now we both know it.

She turns her face toward mine, and her lip trembles. Her hands stay firm on the back of the sofa. "I deserve it." Her whisper is broken. "But sir, please. Please—I can't take—"

I lay a hand on her hair and she lets her head drop back like I've shoved a vibrator between her legs. "No more."

Her eyes fly open. "There has to be...another way."

My God. The laugh I let out is one of genuine surprise. "You're asking me to keep punishing you? I've brought you to my private rooms, away from all prying eyes, and you want more?"

She bites her lip, looks down, nods.

There are *many* other ways to punish a woman, especially one who's begging for it. And I have the sense that another forced orgasm won't be enough for her. Not now, not when everything is so heightened, so razor-sharp. No. It needs to be more...intimate than that.

I have never fallen for a woman. I've never let myself. That doesn't mean I'm without experience...or means. Or tastes.

I move away from her and into the bedroom. Justice doesn't call out after me, and no footsteps pad into the space behind me, so I know she's waiting.

Maybe I have broken her after all.

I press a button at the side of my dresser and a drawer slides open.

The assortment of toys I keep here is enough to provide entertainment enough to sate me. Then I send the women on their way, those whores.

I select a toy that's too big to begin with. I'm only guessing, but it would not surprise me to discover that this is Justice's first experience with this particular kind of punishment. I also take a small bottle of lube. It doesn't need to be *so* harsh. But if I'm going to fuck her—and I am—I should also give her what she needs.

A bit more pain.

Back in the den, Justice is still kneeling on the sofa, her head up and her hands on the back. She has not moved an inch since I left her. As a reward, I put my hand on the back of her neck, below the twist of her hair. "Good girl."

She shudders. "Oh, God."

"And you fought me." I let the laugh linger in my voice. "But you wanted this."

"It's—not right to want this."

"Move your knees back a few inches."

She does.

"Good. Now balance your head on the back of the sofa. You'll need both hands."

She obeys me instantly, but there's a slight hesitation. I was right—she doesn't know what's coming.

"What do I do?" Her voice is so soft. I almost wish she'd fight, but it's delicious knowing that two days of pain from me were enough to make her mine.

Mine.

It's true.

"Reach back and spread your ass for me. As far as you can."

20

*M*y heart beats so hard it feels like it might burst out of my chest and take flight, moving around the room like a macabre little singing bird. Am I hallucinating this? Is this some kind of punishment fever dream? But no, it's not—I reach back and there it is, my punished ass, protesting at my touch. Protest or not, I'll do what he says. It hurts so much I hiss between my teeth, but I get a good grip and spread myself open for him.

This is what I wanted and the sensation of getting it is so heady I could pass out.

But I stay awake, my cheek pressed against the soft back of the sofa, and hold myself in place.

"Christ." It's a rare slip from Cassian. He's normally in control of everything, every aspect of every interaction we have, even when I'm doing my best to upset the balance.

I don't want to upset the balance.

I should want to. I should want to be free, to be independent, but nothing has made me hotter than being on my knees for Cassian Locke. My mind still whirls with what he told me about contracts, about people paying for this to be done to other people, but it's difficult to be shocked when I know what I know. As much as I try to forget it, I still know.

In the dip of my hips above my ass, something cool and slippery drops into place and runs down between my spread cheeks. All my nerves sing with how exposed I am, how open—and the shock of the cold against that secret place makes me shiver.

Cassian's finger against that place makes me shake.

But I want to obey him, more than I've wanted anything else as long as I've been alive. An idea flutters in the corner of my mind like light refracted from a window, or a mirror. That dancing light is the hope that if I do everything just the way he says, he'll...

Hold me.

"Be still."

My body stops moving at his command, even though I thought shivering was one of those uncontrollable things. It's not.

The finger circles, increases in pressure, and forces its way past a barrier.

"It will be easier for you if you relax," he says, his tone matter-of-fact. "But I'm going to do this whether you relax or not."

I suck in a breath. I asked for punishment. He's giving it to me. It's the first time it's been this way.

He works his finger inside, my flesh stretching. It's uncomfortable, and I move my hips side to side, working to accommodate the invasion. The next moment, the finger disappears and I'm rewarded with a sharp slap on the side of my ass.

"Be still."

I know I'll get more than a little slap if I don't follow his rules, so I will myself to be still and concentrate on holding myself open.

One finger. Then...two. That forces a groan from my lips. It's beginning to hurt, the stretching, but then the fingers are gone, and something harder—and wider—takes their place.

"Punishment." His reminder is almost a whisper, but it pales in comparison to the sensation of what's entering my body right now. He pushes it in relentlessly, and it— oh, I can't be silent, I can be still but not silent—it hurts, it's too big. I'm stretched to the limit and just when I think it will go beyond that limit my muscles clamp down on a ridge on whatever it is, this plug, this toy, and I'm left with the pressing fullness of it inside of me. It aches. It burns.

It humiliates me, knowing that he can see this, forced into me, wedged into me, and I am letting him...

And I love it.

I'm dripping wet, the insides of my thighs slick and slippery.

Cassian puts his fingers against my thigh and lets out a low rumble of satisfaction. "A slut for punishment," he says.

"Not—not only punishment."

He strokes a hand down my back. "Oh, I know." He stills his hand. "What happens next isn't punishment." For the first time, he hesitates. "I need you."

21

CASSIAN

I'm not the kind of man who speaks aloud about having a need like this. The words feel foreign in my mouth, but Justice responds to my words like she is lost in the desert and I've given her cool water. Her eyelids flutter closed, long lashes coming to rest on her cheeks, and lets out a little moan.

I'm undone by her.

She's taken everything I have to give her, and still she asks for more. It's like she can see past the suit I hide behind like it's full armor to the raw beating heart buried inside of my chest. And a woman like Justice—she doesn't just look. She's taken a bite of the flesh and made it part of her.

"Hands on the back of the sofa."

Justice releases her grip on her ass and a fresh surge of electric want strikes hard, threatening to take me out at the knees. How it must have hurt to hold herself open like that for me. How I fucking loved the sight of it. She's positioned right where I want her, the plug still visible. It's one size bigger than I thought she could handle, and even if she's whimpering little hissing sounds, even if she's struggling to bear it, she doesn't fight it—doesn't even make a move to step away from the sofa and run.

The release of my belt buckle is a metallic scrape in the air, and Justice's eyes fly open. She doesn't lift her head from where I told her to keep it, but her lips part slightly. She's panting. The scent of her is everywhere, on my fingers, in the air, between her legs, and somehow, though I've done nothing but work to break her since she got here, it's still sweet.

One hand on the small of her back. She leans into my touch, her hips rocking from side to side in tiny movements that seem designed to obey me. I didn't tell her to move. Her obedience is another claw notched into my rib cage. I dip the other hand between her legs and she shifts her knees outward to give me better access.

One stroke of her smooth folds, slick and hot and ready for me, is a direct hit to the last of the standards holding me back. The noise she makes in the back of her throat crumbles the wall I've so carefully built between me and everyone else since I knew what it meant to be my father's son.

There are no words left in my mind to command her, so I take her by the back of the neck and nudge her down onto the sofa. Justice arches back, keeping her face down, her ass in the air, one knee on the verge of slipping off. I climb on behind her and cup my hand back between her legs, clutching all of her in my palm. At first I'm gentle as I circle the swollen nub at the tips of my fingers, but this makes her growl and writhe and twist, so I pin her to stillness by bracing a hand on her hip, and then move my fingers viciously between her legs, increasing the pressure, dipping them inside and spreading that sweetness over her, circling that sensitive place hard enough to make her cry. And come. Without permission. It's something I could punish her for, but instead I catch that new gush of sweetness and lick it off my own fingers.

I hold her still.

I'm throbbing painfully, the head of my cock leaking, and I am at the screaming end of my own wits. Justice is spread wide for me, trembling on her knees, and I thrust myself inside.

For how wet she is, it still takes work. She's so tight and hot that her flesh could sear mine if I didn't want it so badly. If I wasn't prepared. But I am. I've been waiting all my life for this moment.

Justice has her head turned to the side, so I can see her lips moving as I drive myself into her one inch at a time. Does she know she's not making a sound? I put two fingers into her mouth and she closes her lips around them, sucking, a mirror image of the way her pussy is slowly taking me inside. When I pull my fingers out, she releases them with a *pop*. "You'll have to speak up, precious thing."

She digs her nails into the surface of the sofa. "Please—"

Justice is already working to accommodate me, her hips moving side to side, her body opening itself under my invasion, and that one word from her lips...

How will I ever let her go?

With a powerful thrust I'm balls-deep into her, the beautiful sound tearing from her throat like a fucking symphony, and I reward her with a harsh twist of the plug buried in her ass, shoving it in another fraction of an inch. I have an angel on her knees in front of me, an angel offering herself up as a sacrifice, and I'll take it like the vengeful god I've become.

I'm blind to everything in this moment except the sensation of her, clenching and shuddering beneath me, her voice resonating in my ears, her submission the very air that I'm breathing. And now that I'm inside of her, I can't wait any longer. I can't take any more time. I pull myself out so that only the last leaking inch of me is still inside, and then slam back into her. It knocks the breath from her, but she gasps one in to replace it, holding herself there. An offering. The way she's squirming is wordless but it sounds enough like begging to me.

I'm still fucking her, my hips feeling savage even to me, but I reach around her nonetheless and center two fingers over her swollen clit.

"You'll come again for me."

She has to work for the words. "I—can't—"

"You will, or I'll punish you for it." I rub her in small, relentless circles, my other hand tight on her hip. There's nowhere for her to go.

"You're—punishing—me—now—"

"Yes," I growl. "I fucking am."

This makes her become even wetter, makes her spread her legs farther, moan louder.

"I can feel you—where you punished me—"

I know she's not lying, because I'm not holding back. My hips pound against the punished flesh of her ass with every stroke, against the plug, forcing it a little deeper.

"So—cruel—" Justice gasps.

"Not another word from those pretty lips until you come."

It doesn't take her long. Her release is powerful, and I feel it reverberating in waves around my cock. It's too much. It's too fucking much. I keep my fingers on her clit, drawing it out, not caring if it hurts, and she doesn't either because she doesn't so much as beg for me to stop. There are only wordless noises coming from those lips, sweat misting on her skin. It's a wretched, raw thing I've forced from her and the sight of it—the sight of it—

I've never come so hard. It blacks out the corners of my vision and tightens every muscle in my body. For several moments I think I might die like this. It might suck the life right out of me.

It wouldn't be the worst thing, to die like this.

I don't know how much time passes before I pull myself out of her. Spent, Justice collapses to the side, her ass against the back of the sofa. She whimpers, shifting away from it so that the fabric doesn't touch her flesh. Her eyes are closed, her labored breathing even.

My own breathing is not.

I settle it by tracing the line of her jaw with one fingertip, drawing my touch down to her shoulder, then over her collarbone, then between her breasts. I taste the salt that's gathered there and wish I could keep her in my bed tonight. And every night.

But now that I've given in...

"Sir?"

The broken whisper draws my attention back to her eyes. "Yes."

Her lip trembles, but she presses her mouth into a stoic line. "Can I stay with you tonight?"

She's naked, well-fucked, sated. I could pick her up in my arms and put her between my sheets. I could let her sleep on my pillows and wake her myself in the morning.

Another brick slides back into place. The wall rebuilds itself inside my mind.

It doesn't matter what my needs are. What matters is that I'm the one who holds up this world. For my brother...and someone else.

I stroke a hand down to her navel and then force myself to break the connection. Not touching her...it's torture. It's a special punishment all its own. And one that's well-deserved by a man like me. Another man would care for her, after a day like today. After taking her like that. He wouldn't have to outsource the job.

"No."

The corners of her mouth turn down. I'm expecting an argument, a desperate *why*, but Justice pushes herself up instead. One foot after the other, she puts her unsteady legs beneath her and stands, head down, her wrists close together as if they're still bound.

That's when I know she's mine.

22

*E*very step back down the secret passageway from Cassian's rooms to the hallway where I am being held as his prisoner and nothing else is agony.

The way he touched me—the way he spoke to me—I thought...

I'm a fucking idiot.

I'm here to fulfill a contract. To be punished. To be dealt with and discarded. It doesn't matter that I don't know why—my knowing has very little to do with it. It was ridiculous of me to think that this could ever be anything more.

Yet I struggle to keep the tears from falling to my cheeks. With every step, I work harder to blink them away. I can't let them fall. I can't.

It's only that I don't know how I'll live without him. Without...this. And it's filthy and humiliating and it hurts, like how the empty space left behind from the plug still aches. He pulled it out before we left his room and let it fall to the floor.

I can feel everywhere he was inside of me. Everywhere he left his mark.

Cassian presses the code into the keypad outside of my cell and waits while the door opens. A spark inside my gut roars to life—this is where I could fight him. This is where I could prove that I'm still the same girl they had to drag in here kicking and screaming.

But I'm not that girl, am I?

"Justice."

His voice is soft in the hallway, though I still recognize that edge—we're in the hallway now. This isn't some intimate moment. He is Sir and I am nothing.

I turn to face him. Why doesn't he *leave*? I want to throw myself on the bed and swallow back sobs, not face him at the doorway as if we're two people who have never fucked, who have never...

"Tell me where your father is."

"My father?"

"Yes."

"How would I know where he is? I've been held here for days."

The corner of his mouth twists down, and he takes a half step toward me. And I—God help me—I jerk backward. My body knows what will happen if he punishes me for this, and I'm too raw to handle it right now. If he touched me, I'm sure his hands would cut right beneath my skin to the blood in my veins and all of it would belong to him forever.

The thought doesn't seem the least bit dramatic, but the way my heart pounds at the fact of him even an inch closer makes me drop my eyes to the ground. "He's in and out of the city." There's another wrench in my chest. *In and out of the city* doesn't begin to cover what it is my father has done, and it's all tangled up in how good it feels to take the pain from Cassian Locke. "I don't know if he's here or not."

"If he were here, where would he be?" His voice is deadly, and his questions from before rattle around in my mind. *Did you break off an engagement? Cross a man you weren't supposed to?* Was he talking about my father? Is Cassian looking to settle a score that even I don't know about?

The only way I can get answers to my questions is to obey him—I know that much. So I rattle off the address where my father keeps his offices. Where my brother manages those offices when he's not in the city. And where my family lives, on the top three floors of the building.

Cassian gives me a long look.

Then he steps backward, out into the hall, and the next thing I know, the door is closed and locked between us.

I don't wait more than a minute before the door opens again and Mika comes in, a tray in her hands, a few bottles balancing there.

What else is there to do but fall to the pillow and press the side of my face into the cool surface while she works the creams and ointments into my skin, soothing the burn but not the deeper ache?

It's creeping toward dawn when I crawl beneath the flimsy blanket and rest my head on the pillow. Cassian's bed wasn't like this. Obviously it wasn't. Obviously he's not living in a prison. At least part of this building— complex—I don't know what it is—is his home. He didn't let me lay in it, but I don't have to lay in his bed to know he doesn't choose sheets that would tear like paper or pillows pressed flat by so many contracts' heads.

My body welcomes the sleep like an old friend, but I feel like I'm being rocked side to side. It's a little like vertigo. I'm off balance, even as my eyes burn from fatigue. The thing that keeps my dreams at bay are the questions. Will they come for me in the morning, after what happened? Will Cassian still follow through with whatever the contract says? I have no idea how long it's supposed to last. It could be days. It could be weeks. The way he touched me last night makes me think everything could be different when the day finally breaks. Would he really bind me over that bench and make me hurt? After all that? I press my thighs together under the sheet and try not to hope. On the one hand, my ass is still throbbing. Every inch of me aches. But on the other hand, if he stopped...

I don't know if I *want* him to stop. That's how fucked up this is. I fought for my life when they dragged me in here, and now I'm not sure which part of my life I need in order to survive.

At some point in my musings I drift off.

I wake up a little while later, sleep still clouding my brain, to the sound of the door opening.

It wasn't him.

The disappointment rattles in my brain as I lay on the bench on my back, wrists in cuffs, my hands pulled over my head and chained to the wall.

This time...it's different.

The bench had been reconfigured when the woman Mika brought me in and I didn't realize how utterly humiliating it could get until she'd pulled my knees up to my chest and strapped them there, open wide. And it's not like being held in Cassian's grip. I'm here alone, waiting, the cool air leaving its breath between my legs, wondering what fresh hell this day is going to bring.

Punishment, obviously.

Nothing has changed since last night, obviously.

Tears prick at the corners of my eyes and I blink them away. This waiting—this is torture. He must know that. He must not care.

I'm so lost in the particular pain of this that I don't notice the door opening until he's standing next to the bench, grinning down at me, sadistic in his joy.

It's not Cassian.

This must be his brother, judging by the looks of him. He's stockier, with the same fine bones in his face, but there's a cruelty in his eyes that freezes me at my core. The tears dry instantly. He looks me over and I feel that gaze like a knifepoint on my breasts and between my legs. It's useless to tug at the straps holding my knees in this position, but I do it anyway.

"Oh, don't bother." His voice is a twisted version of Cassian's—so similar, yet so wrong. "I'm not enjoying the view." The grin tells me otherwise. "I only wanted to see what he gets up to. In person, I mean. There's always a show available from the cameras. I wanted to see if those screens do it...*Justice*."

He's proud of himself for that one, eyes narrowed, daring me to say something.

I press my lips shut tighter.

He saunters to the bottom of the bench, probably wanting a change of scenery, and stares back between my legs for too long before considering my face. "Did you hear about that king?"

It's bait I don't take.

"You wouldn't, unless my brother told you. And what would he have to say to a contract?" The last word might as well be a curse. "He's so fucking obsessed with propriety. He'd spend days debating if he could tell you at all." He shrugs his shoulders. "I'm not quite so...invested. It was a king in one of those little European countries nobody cares about until something like this happens. Aren't you dying to know?"

I'm dying to be somewhere far away from him. I wish Mika would come back, tell me this is all a mistake, and take me back to the cell. I'd rather be in the cell than with him, like this.

"Got his throat slit." He draws a finger casually across his own throat. "By one of his own advisors. Can you fucking believe it? A coup d'etat. And now the world is wondering where his son is. The *prince*." He shakes his head like he's at a dinner party, discussing something mildly unfortunate. My heart pounds. "Do you think he saw his father die? It's a lot of blood, when throats get slit." He's looking too closely, eyes wandering, then pinning my eyes. One quick step and he's standing over me. "Do you ever fucking say anything? I thought you were supposed to speak when spoken to."

Can he hear it—my heart? It's beating so loud it almost covers his words. I give him one sharp nod.

"What was that?" He cups a hand around his ear.

"Yes." I can barely force the word from my lips.

"It *does* speak. Let's see what else I can make it do." He heads for the wall and I tilt my head back, trying to see what he's doing. A strip of leather bends into my vision. The belt.

"He's got you all trussed up, just for this, I think." That voice—it turns my stomach. Has he been lurking here all along? "It's too bad my brother isn't here to enjoy this."

In one icy moment I understand what his plan is and I strain desperately against my bonds. No. He can't. No. I don't want this, I don't want it—I don't want him to touch me, even if it is using leather. Oh, God, it's something different with Cassian, isn't it? It's so entirely different, and I didn't know it fully until this horrible, sickening moment.

He slaps the belt against his palm while he walks around to his place at the bottom of the bench. The slapping gets louder, and now he's grinning down between my legs, not bothering to look at me. My fear won't be enough for him. Only my pain. And this man—he will not want even the hint of pleasure. This will not be measured. This will not be—

"I've waited long enough." He mutters this almost to himself, and then he raises the belt.

No. *No.* I squeeze my eyes shut, every inch of me trembling, biting back the urge to scream before it even happens—

The door bursts open and I look, I can't help it.

"What the fuck are you doing here, Lysander?"

Cassian.

I could cry from the relief.

He can punish me for hours, all he wants.

Lysander scowls. "You kept her waiting. I was only carrying out the contract."

Cassian strides across the room and whips the belt from his brother's hands. "Get. The. Fuck. Out."

Lysander lifts his chin, like he might fight back, but Cassian's eyes are black with rage and his jaw is set. I press myself back into the bench as if that could possibly hide me.

Cassian pulls the belt tight between his hands and I picture it around Lysander's neck.

Lysander must picture that, too, because he sticks his hands back in his pockets and slinks for the door.

"This isn't finished," Cassian says.

"No, I'm sure it's not," Lysander tosses over his shoulder.

Then he's gone.

Cassian takes a deep breath, closing his eyes.

When he opens them, the rage is hooded beneath the expression I know well.

Sir.

He pulls the belt between his hands, cracking the leather. "That fool doesn't know what to do with a belt." It's a casual comment, almost to himself, and this tiny similarity with his brother sends a shiver down my spine. Then he looks into my eyes. There's no smile there, no comfort, and yet... "But I do."

23

*F*or the first time, I recognize terror in her eyes, pure and unadulterated. And no wonder. This position she is configured in is far more explicit than I had ever imagined. It's not the first time I've demanded that one of the contracts be splayed out in this way, of course. But with Justice...

I looked forward to seeing her like this.

I looked forward to the heat radiating in her eyes, even if I can't ever admit out loud that it's because I know she...trusts me.

Trust isn't supposed to enter into this, but it has, like the ivy that crawls over brick buildings until it can't be taken down without damaging the foundations. No, that's not quite true. It's intimate trust like this that's supposed to be reserved for people with relationships. The families of New York trusted my father, and now they trust me, with toeing the line. They know no one will emerge dead upon fulfillment of one of my contracts.

Justice wasn't sure that she'd survive my brother. The fear is still plain on her face.

I could kill him.

Part of me wants to follow him back to wherever he's taken off to and wrap this belt around his throat, but I can't let him affect me, as much as my rage is streaking white-hot in my veins. I don't let any of it show on my face. That's not part of the contract, and it's not part of what I'm doing to Justice today.

She bites her lip as I step closer.

I shouldn't be looking. Not like this. And God knows how long Lysander stood over her. So I drag my eyes back to her face.

There's a flicker of heat there.

"Punishment." I raise the belt.

Justice sucks in a breath.

I bring it down on the inside of her thigh.

She cries out, writhing in the restraints, or at least trying. There's not enough slack for her to truly move. Mika did her job well.

I keep my hand steady on the belt, painting her creamy thighs with stripe after stripe. The tension I'm carrying in my arms wants to break free, but I'll be damned if I let my boiling anger at Lysander affect her.

Now that he's out of sight and Justice fills my vision, it's easier to stay in control with every moment that passes.

No false moves.

Last night—that was a false move. I can't slip up again.

I drop the belt to the floor and press her knee a fraction of an inch wider. For a moment I allow myself one transgression: I hold my hand a few inches from her pussy, absorbing the heat, even from a distance.

She's soaking.

I didn't have to touch her to know that she was dry when I came into the room. I saw her fear written over every inch of her body.

I bring my palm down on the pink flesh of her thigh. I won't punish her pussy—not now. I saw Lysander's intention in the way he was standing, that fucking disgrace. That kind of punishment rarely enters into the room with contracts. It's far too intimate, and most signers would rather have me humiliate them in other ways.

Justice bears the slaps on her thighs bravely, making little noises of pain as the flesh grows redder and redder under my hands.

I know they're watching.

I felt it most keenly after I put her back in her cell last

night. The empty space in my bed was a stark reminder that this is not only about honoring my father's legacy. Frankly, I could give a damn about my father's legacy. I could forget it all in an instant if it weren't for other ties that bind me to it.

She reminded me of my mother. In some fucked-up way, in a way I can't explain, she reminded me of my mother.

And my mother is not dead.

I don't let myself think of this often, this lie that I tell myself and everyone else in order to survive. But it is a lie. She's not dead. She's in hiding. And I do this because of the Family. My father's Family. An ocean might separate us, but they have eyes everywhere.

This—this is the price I have to pay to keep her safe.

The Family will never have a reason to look for her if I keep this business sacred.

I will, I vow again, bringing my hand down on Justice's upper thigh to mark the deal. Any other contract would be straining to close her thighs, to stop me from doing what I'm doing, but I surface from my thoughts to see an astonishing blush of pleasure blending with the pain on her face.

Her arousal drips down the inside of her thigh.

You're fucking gorgeous, I want to say, but I press my lips closed. Not in this room, not in this room, and not ever again, I can never—

I grit my teeth.

My own flesh is hard, aching, and I have to convince myself otherwise. I have to convince myself that what happened last night can never happen again.

Her knees are nearly touching her chest. She's so exposed to me, with her already punished ass on as much display as her pussy. Taunting me.

I spank it hard.

It surprises Justice enough to draw a scream from her lips, and the sound is utterly delicious.

We are both paying the price.

That cost battles in my mind with the new details I've learned. Was it worth it, leaving her here to meet with her family? It was well outside of protocol, that much I know for sure. I have never paid a personal call to anyone involved with a contract. Not during the duration of the contract and not afterward.

But I did that today.

While she was being washed up.

While she was bound.

While she waited, with my fucking brother ready to undo all my careful work.

Another sharp slap to her ass. Another scream.

It clears my head.

I look down at her, and she's already coming out of it, already pushing a labored breath through pursed lips, cheeks pink. She bears it so fucking beautifully, and it's all for me.

Her eyelashes flutter and her blue eyes meet mine.

Somehow, even after last night, even after the days I've spent punishing her, it's still a shock to me when a contract looks me in the eye. It's a rare occasion. I can count on one hand the number of times it's happened since I took over this work. Since I sent my brother overseas to see firsthand what the Family is capable of.

That fucking bastard. One more misstep and I'll send him back. If he touched *her*—

But he didn't.

This is not the face of a woman destroyed. She may be broken, cracked open for me, but all it's done is strip away the spitting bravado that she had when she first arrived.

I know more about her now.

After the meeting today, I know why she looks at me like this, her eyes begging me for more.

It's against protocol to beg for more. It's against all human reason to beg for more. I should punish her for it— remind her that I'm the one in control, and she can beg all she wants, but she will only ever get what I give her.

It won't make a difference. She already knows.

The corners of her lips turn down, and she shifts her hips in a tiny gesture that opens her even more to my gaze. It's fucking breathtaking in its simplicity, but it breaks me.

All my resolve crumbles.

I want my hand around her throat. I want her fingers between her own legs, or better yet, my mouth.

She hasn't spoken a word, other than to whimper, to scream, to cry while I taught her thighs the meaning of punishment. But now, with my eyes on her face, her lips form a single, silent question.

Please?

In this room, in front of these cameras, I will never give in to her.

I deliver another series of slaps to the insides of her thighs, one after the other, relentless, and then I step back as if she's nothing and no one.

Outside the room, I snap my fingers for Mika, who rushes forward. "Take her back to the cell."

I stalk down the hall, face carefully maintained in a neutral expression. It's only a disguise.

I already know what I'll do tonight.

24

*I*t's a different man who shakes me awake in the middle of the night from a desperate sleep. I was desperate to sleep, and desperate for him to come, and I have tossed and turned in my dreams that featured him coming to this cell, and now he's here.

"Up. Get up."

I stumble over the side of the bed and Cassian takes my elbow, steadying me. What time is it? I look for a clock on the way out of the cell, blinking in the dark like an idiot. There has never been a clock. This place exists outside of time.

The light in the hall is dimmed for the night, but Cassian doesn't need the light to know the way around his own home. I feel where we are, but in the abstract—the only thing that's real is his body next to mine. It seems colder, though, and I shiver as we make our way down that secret passage to his rooms.

The fire crackles in the grate in his den, and I move for the sofa.

"No."

With a gentle tug on my elbow, he leads me in the opposite direction.

My heart leaps into my throat. What is this? An escape...or something better?

He leads us through an open door.

It's his bedroom.

A massive king-sized bed is positioned in the center of the room. A bookshelf lines one wall. A low lamp sits on a bedside table. The scent of him, it's everywhere. Off to one side, I notice a dark-colored doorway that must lead to a walk-in closet. My mouth goes dry at the thought of a naked Cassian walking through here to choose his outfits for the day. This is where he dresses to come punish my naked body.

I have to squeeze my thighs together to keep them from shaking.

He turns to face me and studies me. I must look rumpled. I must look—

"You're gorgeous."

It's not a command, and at first my brain can't process it.

He hasn't cuffed my hands so I can raise one to brush it against my hair. "I'm—"

"Captive. Still gorgeous." He reaches forward and takes my hand away from my hair. I'm going to pass out. He looks down into my palm, as if reading the lines can tell him some secret he doesn't know.

I take in as much of a breath as I can. "You were...so silent today."

He looks back up at me, his dark eyes dancing. "You were not."

I think of the sounds that came out of me and blush, looking down.

"You were perfect." When I look back up into his eyes, his eyebrows are drawn together. "My brother...should never have been there."

"You can make it up to me."

I don't know who we are, having this conversation in this room. But Cassian's face lights up at the words.

One moment he is looking at me like *that,* and the next I'm in his bed.

I'm in his sheets, stretching out with my head on his pillow. I'm swimming in the fresh laundry scent of the fabric and the spice of his own scent, listening to the sound of his clothes dropping to the floor next to the bed.

When he crawls between my legs, I open them for him without a moment's hesitation.

This—*this* will not be punishment. And if it is, it's going to be one I like.

I expect him to take me, but instead he lowers his head between my legs.

Tears gather at the corners of my eyes with his first lick. I never thought—I never imagined this would happen. I never imagined that he would know.

He lifts his head. "I'm sorry."

"Don't—" I press his head back down. "Don't."

Cassian Locke is a master of devouring pussy. Mine, in particular. He holds my thighs open, the flesh tender beneath his thumbs, and licks and sucks, every movement worshipful and exacting. I know he's not sorry for what he did to me. He's only sorry that his brother had the chance to ruin it. Four days ago, it wouldn't have made a difference which man stepped into the room. And now—now—

I come hard into his mouth. He won't let my hips go, like he *has* to taste this, and he laps up my juices until I come a second time. Then he crawls on top of me and thrusts inside of me in a powerful sweep, my swollen entrance clenching around him.

This version of Cassian between my legs is like nothing I've ever seen. He's a wonder of the world. Every inch of him is toned and taut, his waist nipped in with so many muscles I can't help but scrape my fingertips over them. The sight of him in the low light of that little lamp winds me up, which should be impossible because I am already at my limit for orgasms of that caliber. It doesn't seem to matter when he's fucking me to his own climax, his face pressed into my collarbone, all of him laid out against me. I can feel him, and it destroys me.

When he's finished with me, he turns on his side, throwing his arm across my waist, and this draws a tear from the corner of my eye and it trickles down my cheek.

"Tell me what you need."

He's asking me if I need pain. But this pleasure—somehow, it's pain enough. Because I don't know if it'll ever happen again.

I shake my head.

A silence follows that's almost long enough for me to fall asleep.

"It's not your fault."

I don't know what he means, but his shift in tone has me instantly and fully awake. He runs his fingers absently through my hair.

"What?"

I'm still not used to speaking to him like this, but it doesn't matter. I have to know what he's talking about.

"I went to visit your father."

My stomach turns. "Did you see him?"

"No. I met with your brother."

"That's—" My mouth is dry, and I'm aware more than ever of how openly I'm sprawled on the bed. I cross one knee over the other. "What did he say?"

"The payment for your contract?"

I nod.

"It came from your family trust."

"What does that—" I press both hands to my forehead. "What does that mean?"

"From what I gather, they were the ones to arrange the contract. It wasn't to settle a dispute. Or—it wasn't to settle a dispute with an outside family." He grimaces. I never took Cassian to be the type to have feelings about what other people wanted out of these arrangements, but they're written all over his face.

The meaning sinks in.

"They did this to me."

His silence is enough of an answer. Now I know—I know why he couldn't speak to me in the room today. Not even to play his part. He was keeping all this inside his head.

"I know what he does."

"My father?" The words are a soft rasp, and my stomach

folds in on itself. I know what he does, too. But now it's present in the air between us, that terrible knowledge. The way my father makes his money. The way he earns his power. "How?"

"My own father kept records. I didn't think to look until after the meeting." He shakes his head. "That's where I was when Lysander—" He must think better of saying anything further because his voice trails off. "I know what he does."

I can't look at him.

I turn my face to the side, hiding from him. Cassian reaches out and settles two fingers under my chin, turning me back to him. I can't look away.

"What could possibly make you ashamed in front of a man like me?"

I can hardly take in a breath. Am I hallucinating? Am I seeing this man before me as...the man? Not the towering figure in a suit, the menacing one with a belt?

When the oxygen finally forces its way into my lungs, I know there's no room for anything but honesty.

"I was part of it." This is the truth that keeps me bent over that bench instead of fighting it all the way down. I deserve it. I do. I can't even pretend otherwise. He's stripped me of my ability to do that. "Complicit. I...lured people."

"You knew what he was doing?"

All those years, during my childhood, I had no idea. I knew there were certain things we didn't talk about. Certain things that were better not to know. But it wasn't until I turned sixteen that he started using me as part of the business. It's like a permanent stain on my skin. "I didn't know the full extent until a few months ago. And once I knew—" Bile rises in my throat and I force it back down. "I was going to run away with my boyfriend. He was the only one who knew about our plan, and—"

"He gave you up."

I never would have believed him. Not until now. But his voice is a quiet truth.

"My brother." I shudder at the thought of him, so like my father. "Did he tell you about my sister?"

"No." Cassian's eyes are wary. I can see why, with a brother like his.

"She's gone." I turn my head to the side and wipe another tear on the pillow. "I don't know if it's like this—" I gesture vaguely toward the door. "Or if it's—better, or if it's worse, I don't—" A sob fights its way to my lips, choking me. Cassian strokes a hand down the side of my cheek. "I don't know." My sister. She's been gone four months. She never said a word about what she had to do, but I knew. I knew, because I had to do it, too. Maybe she escaped, but maybe...

"You'll be all right. Once the contract is fulfilled, and you leave, you can look for her—"

My blood runs cold, like cracking ice. "You said my father wasn't there."

"No."

My father is the only one with a weakness. At least, a potential weakness. Maybe he was the one who signed that contract. But if it's only my brother—

"And you're still going to send me back?"

Cassian's mouth is a thin, hard line. "Those are the terms."

"So what?" I won't cry anymore. I swear it to myself.

"With what your father knows, he could bring me down. Your brother could. They could crush my reputation, and my business." He's leaving something out. Could he care that much about his brother?

"But I thought—" I can't bring myself to say it. I thought the bed was a sign. Now I see that he's meant it as a parting gift. A consolation prize. It's too much to take. I should get up and leave, right now, but instead my body responds to the crushing blow with a wave of fatigue. My arms and legs collapse heavily against the sheets.

Cassian leans down and presses a kiss to my lips. It feels like an apology, but it's faint—or maybe I'm fading. I wait for him to shake me awake, to take me back to the cell, but he only pulls up the blankets to tuck around me.

"It's all I can do," he whispers. Or maybe I'm dreaming it. I'll never know.

25

CASSIAN

*L*ess than forty-eight hours remain in the contract when I walk into the room and find Justice bound over the bench. Mika has always been meticulous in her work, and today is no exception. I can tell she's scrubbed Justice's skin to a pink that verges on overdone, then covered it in a lotion that leaves her supple. If I were to touch her, my own skin wouldn't catch on hers. She's a blank slate, ready for punishment. Even the marks from the four strokes of the cane have faded nicely. Mika tended to that, too.

Justice doesn't look at me as I enter the room. She doesn't so much as try to turn her head, only keeps her eyes trained on the wall in front of her.

I stride over to the rack on the wall, listening to her breathe behind me and try to calm my thoughts. I was calm before I saw her, but now...

It's like there's a fire under her skin. Only I can't see it.

I'll go back to basics. I'll start with my hand.

I move around next to Justice and put my hand on the small of her perfectly arched back. She gives no indication that she realizes I'm there—doesn't startle, doesn't move. I watch her for long enough to know that she doesn't even flick her gaze over to mine, only stares blankly ahead.

I don't fucking like that.

"Forty strokes to begin," I tell her. It's a high number, given what she went through yesterday, given what I've put her through since she got here. But Justice doesn't protest. She looks down at the leather surface of the bench. "How many of those do you think you can tolerate?"

It's a direct question, and her lips curve down as she decides on an answer. "All of them."

I stroke my fingers down her back toward the cleft of her ass, not entirely gently. I want a reaction out of her. "Should we settle on fifty, then?" I hate the sneering sound of my voice, but I don't know who this woman is. The fire is so far beneath the surface that none of the light escapes.

"That's up to you." Flat. Unemotional.

No. She won't be like this. Not when she's mine.

I press down on the small of her back, a more tangible

reminder that she can't go anywhere without my blessing, and bring my hand down hard on her ass.

Justice throws her head back, the twist of her hair shaking, but she doesn't make a sound. I rain down several more blows with the same intensity. Her bottom blooms red beneath my palm but she doesn't make a sound until twenty strokes in, and it's nothing like what I've come to expect from her. There's no pleasure in it. I never thought I would be waiting for pleasure mixed with pain in a contract's voice. I never fucking cared.

Thirty.

Forty.

Tears leak out from the corners of her eyes, spilling over her cheeks, making her eyes a deeper blue than I've ever seen. But there's no subtle rock of her hips, no attempt to grind her clit against the surface of the bench. By this point in any session she's lost control of her ability to hold still no matter how tightly Mika has bound her. No matter how tightly *I've* bound her. It's been as essential to her being as breathing.

Now, stillness.

I try to thrust away the hot, sick rage that fills my stomach and creeps up into my lungs, but it's twisted itself up into my organs like a cancer. It's fucking pathetic. Emotion like this—it's never supposed to come into this room, and over and over again Justice has clawed it out of me.

Fifty.

She's still whimpering, but the moment silence reigns in the room she tries to tamp it down, swallowing hard on the cries. She takes in a shuddering breath and releases it slowly, her head hung low, like a woman who is only enduring and finds nothing else in this.

This is what it must have been like to be run through with a sword. The impact. The shock. And the cold, spreading realization that it's a fatal blow.

Only my mind won't accept it for that kind of wound. Heat sears up around the entry point, covering it over, a fever that reaches all the way up and into my brain.

Justice takes another breath and her body stills. She lifts her face from the bench and stares ahead at the wall.

Something inside of me snaps. Is it a rib? An artery going into my heart?

I'm at the wall in an instant, the belt in my hand in another instant. I don't trust myself with the cane, with anything else. I bend down so I'm at the level of her face, close enough to see that her chin is trembling. She must have her teeth gritted shut. It's something.

But it's not enough.

"Punishment," I whisper, and it seems the word goes straight to her core because her body quakes. I can see in her eyes that she's struggling to get it under control. It's in this interval that I move back around behind her to the optimal position.

This time, I don't give her a number.

This time, I bring the belt down without warning.

Once.

Twice.

Three times.

Hard enough to make her howl.

An alarm sounds in the back of my mind, blaring, drowning out even the sound of my shattering heart, a light blinking red in the corner of my vision. I'm having an out-of-body experience, watching my arm come down again and again, feeling the minute contractions of the muscle in my shoulder from far away. Watching the red on her skin deepen, and deepen.

No.

Do I say the word out loud? I don't know. It rings in my ears, along with ragged breathing that I recognize a moment later as my own. All I know is that I've stepped back. I've dropped the belt to the floor.

Justice is crying as prettily as she ever has, tears like falling rain, silent sobs. I've pushed her too far. But it wasn't on the bench today that I did it. It was last night. I wonder if she remembers waking to tell me everything Lysander said before I entered the room. He used me against her, that bastard. He told her about a king being murdered, a son in exile—he made her think that I was never coming for her. In a way, he was right. I can never come to her rescue in the way that she wants, and for the first time in my life, it's tearing me apart.

This is a fact that can never be spoken aloud in this room. My palm aches to stroke her hair, to get down on my knees next to her and take back what I've done. Take back every cruel promise I made to her last night.

If it was only me riding on this contract, if it was only me riding on this business, I would. I would have given it up long ago.

I swipe my sleeve over my forehead and stumble numbly to where the chain connects her cuffs to the wall.

"What—" A broken whisper.

"Silence."

I release her from her bonds by myself.

All of this is against protocol. I never take her back to the cell by myself. I step outside and let Mika handle the aftermath. And my hands are always steady. Steadier than this.

Justice doesn't know what to do, hesitating on the bench even though there's nothing holding her there. I put my fingers on the cuffs and tug at her wrists, forcing her to her feet. She looks down at the floor, still crying. It tastes so fucking bitter not to touch her. It tastes so fucking bitter that it had to be her, that it had to be now. I don't want to leave her here like this.

So instead I lead her outside, turning to force her in front of me. Down the hall, Mika is flat against the wall, eyes wide. The moment she sees us both step outside she disappears through the door, leaving it to close behind her with a whisper.

At the cell I enter the code, then take Justice's elbow and push her inside. The searing beat of my own heart terrifies me. It fucking terrifies me. How can a person breathe like this?

She stands in the center of the cell, head down.

"Look at me."

Her eyes snap up, no longer blank, just aching.

"Forgive me." I hiss the words between gritted teeth.

"No."

A cannonball, straight to the gut. I step forward so that I'm standing on the threshold, fist balled at my side. "You can't hold this against me."

Wide eyes, more tears. This is water torture. She must know it. "I can. You're—" I wish she'd sob out loud. It would be easier to take than this. "You're what I need and you're throwing me away."

It's such a naked admission that it makes her more open and vulnerable to me than when she was flat on her back on the bed, my hand clasped around her neck. *I'm* what she needs? I can't be. She has no idea what she's saying.

My heart breaks into two ragged halves, each one tumbling to a different side of my chest.

"I'm fulfilling the agreement." The words puncture like daggers in my throat.

"You're sending me back to a monster. To...more than one monster." Her eyes shine with something else, a flare that peaks and fades.

Breathtaking. "I'm a monster. Can't you see that? I can't fucking save you."

"Then don't." Her chin trembles again, and I'll be damned if I don't want to press my thumb against it, press my lips against hers. "Let me die here with you instead of through slow torture with them." A deep breath that does nothing to steady her. "My father—my brother—they sent me here. One of them sent me here. And they won't hesitate—they won't ever stop—"

"Come with me."

Hope. Such an innocent, naive hope lights up her eyes, it almost kills me on the spot. "Where?"

"To my rooms." I try to communicate in this sentence that the rooms are all I can offer, and it's only for one night.

I don't say it out loud. She seems to understand it anyway.

The light fades from her eyes, leaving them as blank as before. A last tear falls down her cheek. I hear it when it hits the floor. I didn't know a single water droplet could be so loud.

She shakes her head.

No.

"Are you refusing me?"

Those eyes flash one more time, lightning in blue. "I don't really have a choice, do I? I have to do what you say."

I can tell by the way her shoulders curve toward mine that she wants to obey me. I've seen what it does to her body. I've seen how she revels in that pleasure. My other hand balls into a fist. I release both of them, but it takes all the effort in the world.

I could make her come with me. I could take her by the wrists, take those bound hands, and—

But it's not what I want.

"Step forward."

She does, tentative.

"Wrists."

I undo the cuffs and hang them on the hook just outside the door.

"Come with me."

Justice drops her wrists in front of her, head drooping as if her only obsession is the floor at her feet.

I don't want to force her. Not this time. Not on the last night.

"Do you—want to come to my rooms?" The question feels flat and strange on my tongue. I'm not used to asking.

A single shake of her head. That's all I get.

No.

No, no, no.

26

I know it's the end when Cassian comes to get me himself.

The morning started like all the others, with Mika taking me to be bathed. Did I imagine it, or was she gentler this time? I caught her watching me, like there was some clue hidden in my face, twice.

When it was over, she brought me back to my cell.

I thought I would be relieved, when this ended. When I was brought here I didn't know if it *would* end, but now the ending is a far worse prospect than being here.

I was awake all night, thinking of what Cassian said and what it means.

I've had enough time to consider all the possibilities, and the one I've settled on is the most dangerous of all.

My brother was always the one who was going to take over my father's business. It's that way for most fathers and sons in our circle. My father has been unique in the way he used his daughters—most men only use them to make alliances by marriage. They still have a fetish for feudal England.

That's not my brother's plan for me.

My father never spoke to Tripp. At this point, he can't possibly still consider himself my boyfriend. What Cassian said must be true, because nobody else knew where I'd be that night. Nobody else knew where we were supposed to meet.

The person who knew Tripp the most, other than me, was my brother.

They were friends.

The realization came upon me after I'd cried out all my futile disappointment into the flimsy pillow last night. Tripp knew Hector. They saw each other on social occasions, and at one of the parties I threw they spent several minutes huddled in the corner, leaning in close to talk.

Why would I have thought twice about that?

Tripp can't possibly consider me his girlfriend anymore, because I know what Hector would have given him in exchange for...me.

I can't go back.

I can't go back, because when I was bent over that bench,

the belt coming down on my ass in white-hot stripes, it came to me that Cassian is wrong.

He thinks these contracts aren't about emotion. He thinks they're about settling scores and walking away, his hands still clean. And maybe it is that way, for him. Maybe his mind discards what he knows about each of the women he punishes and breaks, and it's as if they never existed.

But to them—to *us*—it will always be as if he existed. As if he owned us.

It's twisted, how much I still want to belong to him. It's beyond fucked up. I have the sense that other women— they're glad to be free, but they'll always watch themselves. They'll always wonder if they'll have to return here. I bet most of them never do. I bet most of them fall in line.

My father used my sister and me as bait, as lures, to get the men he was paid to target to a clean room with no witnesses.

Cassian's business is punishment. My father's business is death. And I was the beautiful thing that led men there.

If Hector has his way, I'll do more than take men by the hand. I can feel it in my bones.

I can't go back.

At first I think he's taking me to release me when he opens the door to the cell, but he holds up the cuffs. And like a good girl, I go and hold out my wrists. It's so sick, the relief I taste on my tongue. If he punishes me again, I've bought another hour with him, and not out there.

In the room, a chair sits squarely in the center, like it did the first night I was here. I hardly look at it, expecting him to take me to the bench, but he doesn't.

He sits in the chair, and waits.

I'm the sacrifice, and I'll have to offer myself.

I want to offer myself.

My heart breaks.

Wordlessly, I bend myself over his lap.

I don't want to give myself over to him, but the moment his legs press into my belly and his hand goes over my waist, holding me still, I do.

The crying—there's been enough crying. I have cried more tears than I ever have. But they sting my eyes nonetheless.

There's no growl from Cassian, no number of strokes, no reminder that I'm here to be punished—to pay for my sins. He will still punish me. It doesn't matter that I've already paid.

Why does it feel like my chest is caving in? Why does it feel like my first love is breaking up with me in the corner of the prep school courtyard?

He rubs a palm over my ass, centering it, and I brace my

toes against the floor, lifting up for him. My tears form a miniature puddle on the other side.

With the first strike, they triple.

I want him so much.

I want *this* so much.

I want to be held over his lap, and for the pain of the punishments to wash away the guilt that chokes me for all I've done in my life. One, two, three, four. I want a hundred. I want a thousand. I'll never have this again, and I want it to last. What other man could understand the filthy part of my soul that needs this? What other man has the same darkness inside of him? He's the only one who knows the depth of my need. He's the only one, only one, only one.

It's over too soon.

My ass burns and stings. I'm sure it's pink. My toes are no longer braced against the floor—I hang over his lap, a puppet with her strings cut. He could never break me by keeping me here. He can only break me by letting me go.

He rubs his hand over my ass. His palm feels cool, but I know it's mostly that my skin is hot. A sob heaves my chest. No. No, this can't be—

Cassian slides his fingers between my legs.

My toes are instantly against the floor again, lifting toward him, giving myself, and I clap my own hand over my lips, covering the gasp. I don't have to see his face to know this is a gift. An awful, terrible, wonderful gift.

He pins me there, fingertips stroking, working, gathering my juices. It takes no time until I'm rocking my hips against him. It's sheer pleasure, all twisted up with my broken heart.

"Yes," he hisses, the word barely louder than a breath, and I shatter on his fingers, biting into my own knuckle to keep quiet.

He holds me there until I settle back into stillness, the aftershocks of release still rushing through my veins.

There's a soft knock at the door.

Cassian lifts me from his lap, standing me next to the chair, and rises. I take in the movement like it's the last sight I'll ever see. Those strong lines, hidden from me by a suit that looks like it was made for him. I'm seized with jealousy for that suit. It gets to touch his skin.

He lets Mika in. She carries a dress folded over her arm and a pair of flats. They're not mine—they cut the dress off my skin on the first day I was here and I don't know when I lost my shoes—but it's a flimsy black dress, a halter top. Too cold for fall. It's the equivalent of what I came here in, which strikes me as both mean-spirited and symmetrical, in a terrible kind of way.

Cassian takes the clothes from Mika and nods toward the door. She walks out without a word.

He pulls the dress over my head. No bra. No panties. His protocols are meant to humiliate until the last possible moment. I can admire his dedication, even though I want to fall in a heap at his feet and beg him for mercy.

Then he puts the flats at my feet, and I step into them.

There are no words.

There are simply no words.

My pulse throbs in my veins. I thought I knew fear the night those men put me into the back of that car. I didn't know fear at all.

He looks down at me, his dark eyes filled with an unnameable emotion.

When he raises a hand to stroke it against my cheek I don't bat it away. No—it only strikes a match of hope at the center of my chest. I raise my face to his.

He doesn't kiss me.

Cassian leads me to the stairs.

I haven't thought much of that other door at the end of the hallway—the one they carried me through. It never seemed like it would be an option for me. Cassian strides toward it with his head held high, and something about the way he moves reminds me of a man going toward the gallows. Not that I've ever seen a man going to the gallows, except in the movies. And it's not him who will have to survive this. It's me.

I press my lips together, willing myself not to say a word. I've faced all of this and come through it. I won't fall apart now.

I tell myself that, but at the bottom of the staircase, my body revolts.

Cassian reaches for the handle of the door and I jerk backward, moving up one step.

"No. Please."

The words fall on deaf ears. He turns to look at me, a slight irritation curving his mouth. "It's time."

"Please."

He takes me by the elbow.

I pull back against him. He's too strong—it will never work. I can't manhandle the both of us up the stairs, so I yank my arm out of his hand and twist away. Maybe if I can get to the top, he'll let me stay—maybe if I can get to the top, I can bargain with him—

He wraps his arms bodily around me, and God help me, I am so desperate for his touch that I let it happen.

But it's not a hug. He's not holding me close for comfort. He lifts me toward the door effortlessly, without even a deep breath, and shoves it open.

The cold is bracing. How did it get so cold in—what, five days? It wasn't this cold when I left the club, and it filters through my dress like it's made of paper. It might as well be. Cassian puts me out on the sidewalk and turns me to face the street.

I whirl around and grab for his sleeve, feeling the most pathetic I've ever felt, like a little girl grabbing for her father's hand, but he is not my father, and my father wouldn't save me anyway. He pulls his sleeve away so I can't touch it, and for some reason this is the thing that breaks me all the way down.

"No. *Please.*"

"It's my family." His beautiful face is twisted. He has to be struggling. He has to know this is a mistake. "There are people who watch. I can't—" He shakes his head. "I can't. You don't understand."

"I understand," I shout at him, like shouting can make any difference.

"It's time to go." This time his eyes are painted with pain. "Go, Justice."

I spin around in the street, looking for which way to run, knowing even as I do that it's going to be pointless. Someone has arranged all this. Someone will be waiting for me. And if they get me back to my family's home, it'll all be over. I know it. Hector will keep me on my knees and worse for an endless parade of men, and my father will let him, because that's the way they are.

I'm still looking for a way out when I spot the SUV.

I'd know it anywhere.

It's one of my father's fleet, used by his men.

I gasp in a breath and turn back toward Cassian, but he's already gone, his hand on the door.

"Cassian—" It's a strangled scream.

He doesn't turn back.

He pulls the door open and steps inside.

I sprint for the door, one of my shoes coming off in the process. As my hands close around the metal handle, he reaches up for something, a switch of some kind, and I feel the click of the lock reverberate through my palms.

"Cassian!" This time it's a real scream.

He turns away from the window.

I scream again.

He's gone.

27

CASSIAN

$\mathcal{E}$very step up the stairs, with her screams ringing in my ears, taunts me with exactly who I am.

A slave.

A slave to the legacy my father signed me up for. A slave to the eyes and ears watching me from across the ocean. It's worth it to them, to own me. All their interests are bound up inextricably with the people here who live in high-rises, who fight and fuck and claw at one another and want retribution afterward. And I'm the one who gives it to them. They don't want to get their hands dirty. They don't want blood spilled, unless it's in my punishment room, and that's all I'm ever going to be.

I'm the second signature on a contract. And sometimes, I'm not even that. I'm just the hand that delivers justice. For everyone except me.

Have I ever walked up these stairs, like this, before? No.

Not even one time. I've never taken a contract back out. I've never left one there, with her fate lurking in the street.

I've never cared.

Never once have I allowed myself to care. Because caring about contracts is a recipe for disaster.

I get to the top of the stairs and punch in the code at the top, blindly, so haphazardly that I get it wrong twice before the damn thing opens. The hallway itself guts me. It's like she's left her scent everywhere she touched, everywhere she's been, and I will never be able to see this carpeting or that doorway without thinking of her again.

So I don't look. I just keep going, through one hall, down another, another, and all the while she's screaming for me in the back of my mind.

I only discover where I'm going when I get there and find Lysander sprawled in front of the bank of monitors, his feet up on the desk, scrolling through his phone. He glances up at me, desultory, sighing, useless. He doesn't know anything and he never will, because I've fucking saved him from that, like I saved him from everything else. "Did you take that last one out to the curb? We need to clear out the room for something worth more money."

I'm on top of him before I know what I'm doing, hauling him up by the front of his collar. He twists in my grip. "What the fuck, Cash?" A leering smile spreads across his face. "Did you fall for the bitch? No, you never would. It's below our *standards*."

I'm as surprised as he is when my fist makes contact with the side of his face. I release him just after the blow lands, dropping him back on his ass in the seat and leaning in close. "Say another word about her, Lysander. Say it."

His hand is on his jaw, his eyes are latched on mine, and I can hear his breath in his throat. But he doesn't say anything.

He's in here, and despite what I've done to him, he's still safe. He'll be all right. The bruise will heal. He will forever depend on my mercy, forever rely on me not sending him back to the Family to have a lesson in the way they do business.

But with Justice...

What the fuck am I sending her back to?

And what else matters if I do?

Lysander's eyes turn wary, like he's waiting to see if I'm about to kill him. I must look murderous. I could go farther than I've already gone, but I won't, because it's a waste.

It's all a waste, if I don't have her. It's all a waste, if she's not breathing, if she's not living, if not with me than somewhere else on this earth.

I put her out by the curb. I did what he said. Like garbage, waiting to be collected. And if she's sane, she'll never forgive me for that.

I grab Lysander's head in both my hands and he pulls back. "Thank you, you stupid bastard." I'm hardly done spitting the words into his face before I'm moving again, tearing for the door like getting to her is the only thing that will save me.

Because it is. The only thing that will save me. No—not even that. I'm not worried about being saved. God can crush me beneath his heel, for all I care, he can blow me away with a tornado or rip through my innards with a gunshot, as long as I can get to her.

Mika is in the hall when I burst through and flattens herself against the wall, her face white. Has she ever seen me run? Have I ever run through the house before? Have I ever had a reason? The air burns in my lungs, but it's not because running is particularly taxing. It's because something is threatening to rise in my throat, and I don't know what it is, but I'm not letting it into the world. A sob? A scream? It doesn't matter.

I fly down the stairs two at a time, then three. How long has it been since I left? A minute? Two? If I'm too late—

I burst through the door and out into the cool. The fall is turning, icing into winter, and the cold finds every available seam to exploit. I took her to the left.

There's no one there, just evening fading into darkness.

But to the right—

A black SUV is pulled up to the curb.

There are two men.

There is Justice, in a dress worse than the one she arrived in. It's an awful thing that doesn't deserve her.

And she is not going quietly.

Another scream splits the air. It's not my name. She doesn't think I'm coming. It's a curse, followed by another, followed by pure rage.

I run.

They don't see me coming until I'm almost there.

"Hey, this guy—"

The first man doubles over with a *whoosh* of breath from my fist buried in his gut. I'm taller than both of them, but the only advantage I have here is surprise. I don't know if they're armed. I'm assuming they are. And I'm not. But my fury is enough. It has to be enough.

The second guy has his hand locked on her wrist and the sight of it makes my last vestiges of self-control combust.

I wrap my fist around his wrist and squeeze. The dumb-fuck is staring, open-mouthed. What kind of people do they hire these days for retrieval?

"Let go," I growl in his face.

He goes for his pocket.

I go for his nose.

It shatters under the heel of my hand and I feel him release his grip. Justice stumbles backward.

"Fuck," says the second guy, blood streaming from his nose.

I position myself between her and them.

The first guy, he has some sense. "Let's get the fuck out of here."

The second spits a mouthful of blood. "Without her? Mr. Hector—"

"The boss'll never find us if we take another job."

My heart pounds. To hurry along their decision making, I take a step closer. The second guy reaches for his pocket again.

"Reach any farther and I'll kill you." I put my own hand at my back. I've already broken his nose.

He decides I'm not worth it.

I watch until the doors of the SUV are closed, then whirl to Justice.

She's not there.

She's hurrying down the street, getting away from all of us.

"Justice!"

She doesn't hesitate at the sound of my voice.

"Please!"

That stops her where she stands, and she turns, the autumn wind whisping her hair around her face.

"What do you want?"

She's crying. I can see the tears from halfway down the block. I don't dare take another step toward her in case she bolts.

"You."

I let the word ring across the space between us.

"You left me out here," she yells back.

"I left everything else behind."

"I just want to go home." She wraps her arms around herself. The dress is too flimsy for the cold. "But I don't know where that is."

I open my arms.

She waits.

"I love you."

"You don't even know me. You don't know how many people I've—"

"I love you."

"I love you."

I don't care who's listening. I don't care that I'll need several lifetimes with her in order to know all of her secrets. I don't care. I don't care. My heart seizes. If she goes the other way, I'll go back. I'll go back to the life I had. I'll do it until the day I die. I'll be an empty man.

Justice takes one hesitant step, then another, and then she's running, barefoot, across the concrete, and she doesn't stop until she collides with me, sobbing, alive.

I can't hear what she's saying, she's crying so hard, her teeth chattering. She tips her face up toward mine and I kiss her through her tears, tasting blood. She must have bitten one of her lips when they tried to take her away.

She says it again.

"I love you."

"God."

"It's stupid."

"Nothing could ever be more stupid. I'm a dangerous man."

"Please don't leave me out here again."

"Never."

I take off my jacket and wrap it around her shoulders, then reach down to her waist to pluck out my phone. We're going to need a car, and a plane, and I'm going to need to draw from a private account. I'll never touch the family accounts again, because we need to disappear. Maybe forever.

Justice presses her body into me, solid and warm despite

the cold in the air, as I dial the number and speak into the phone.

We only have about a minute to wait. "We're done paying the price," I tell her.

"I'd pay it again."

I kiss her hair. "Your debts are settled."

"You still owe me." A flicker of a smile crosses her face, and it lights up my entire soul.

"I'll pay," I tell her again, and I see the car at the end of the street. We're thirty seconds from freedom. "Always."

EPILOGUE

JUSTICE

"*I*stria," Cassian says as the church bell tolls, rolling over the peninsula. I'm standing at a window looking over the bay, watching the sun play over the waves and reveling in the fact that he's here in the same room with me.

He hasn't left my side in six months, but the sensation of having him nearby never gets old.

"What about it?"

Cassian comes up behind me, running his hands down over my arms and pressing his lips into the side of my neck. He likes it when I wear my hair up like this, just so he can kiss me like this. The heat of his mouth makes goosebumps rise under his touch. "It seems like an imaginary name from a peninsula."

I lean back into him, feeling his weight and warmth. "I like it."

He takes in a deep breath and lets it out. "You seem lost in thought, precious thing."

"I was thinking of—" I was thinking of New York, and how I don't care if I never see the city again. There are some things I miss about it. My favorite little restaurants, for one. But other than that... "I was thinking of how much I like being here with you."

"Like?" Cassian teases. "If you don't like it, I have ways of convincing you otherwise."

That brings a blush to my cheeks and a smile to my face. "The windows are open."

"Not all punishments need to be loud."

I press my thighs together under the fabric of my dress. Cassian, it turns out, isn't such a glutton for pain. He is a glutton for pleasure. Me, on the other hand? I like them both in equal measure. Luckily, he knows how to give it to me.

I know he wouldn't hesitate to open the case he carries with the various toys that can make my toes curl along with his touch, but I lick my lips and try to remain a responsible lady. "I thought we were meeting someone."

"We are."

It's the first time in all these weeks that he's wanted us to be in a specific place at a specific time. At first, we disappeared into Europe. He explained to me on the plane ride over that the Family his father reports to is a lot more sprawling than blood relatives, and they watch him most closely in New York. But they also have tendrils everywhere. It makes more sense, the king who was killed by his own adviser. According to Cassian, the Family had representatives there, too.

I asked him why we were getting so close. It felt like we were flying right into danger.

"Keep your enemies closer," he said. "Besides, they won't think to follow me around Europe. Now that my brother is in charge—" His face darkened at that, and I reached for his jawline, running my fingers over his skin.

"I know."

"He's not who I would have chosen." I didn't need to spend a long time with Lysander to know that what Cassian did out of duty, Lysander would do out of cruelty. It won't be long before the business collapses under the weight of his thirst for power and pain. When that happens—

When that happens, we'll worry about it. Until then, Cassian shifts his weight from foot to foot behind me.

"Yes. There is someone I'd like you to meet."

A thrill of excitement centers at the back of my neck, but it's tempered with wariness. "You're not joining the Family, are you? This isn't—"

He laughs, a low rumble that sounds like desire. "No. I

would only do that in the most drastic of circumstances. And standing on a balcony with you, precious thing, is not a desperate circumstance." He pauses. "I only wanted to make sure you were relaxed before our...meeting."

I don't know what this could be about. He told me his father returned to the fold of the Family years ago, then died of a heart attack, so it can't be that kind of introduction.

He lifts his wrists in front of both our faces. "We should go down."

We go out of the little apartment with its fine furniture and down to the street level of Rabac. Cassian looks both ways and must see something that makes him comfortable. I've never caught a glimpse of the protection he's hired, but that's all right—I wouldn't recognize them anyway. He rotates through the staff at different intervals. Then he turns right, following the street as it winds toward the bay.

Rabac seems like a fairy tale name as much as Istria, but I know it's more my fairy tale mood than anything else. Though the setting does quite a bit to encourage that image. The sparkling bay, the fishing village, the way we have to come up a steep hill each night to our villa. The streets aren't too crowded with tourists in the spring, but the weather is warmer each day. Soon it will be summer.

I'm about to ask Cassian if we'll stay for the next season when he turns and enters the door of a little cafe tucked into a courtyard off the street. He turns back and extends his hand to me, and I take it.

"Was *meeting* code for lunch date?" I'm still not over that, either. The fact that he can take me on dates. The fact that he wants to. How many women get to live two lives?

"We'll be having lunch." He gives me a little half smile, and for the first time I realize he's nervous.

At the back of the courtyard is a table underneath an umbrella. I think Cassian's going to walk right past it, but he stops. I'm behind him, waiting to see where he's going, but when I lean around I see there's a woman seated at the table in a flowing blue dress.

She turns, and with a shock I recognize Cassian's features on her face. The same nose, the same dark eyes, the same regal lines.

Her eyes are brimming with tears.

"My son," she says, and then she rises on tiptoe and wraps her arms around his neck.

His mother.

I thought she was dead.

It's clear to me now.

She was hiding.

He was hiding *her*.

This is the reason for everything—for the business, for the insistence on duty and protocol—everything.

After a long embrace, he straightens, taking her by the elbow and stepping to her side. "Justice, this is my mother, Eline. Mama—" The word in his mouth squeezes my heart so tightly I can hardly breathe. "This is the love of my life, Justice Danes."

I see in her eyes that she understands everything, even without him saying a word.

Eline comes forward and folds me in her arms. She smells warm and sugary, like the air around us, like safety. Like home.

When she pulls back, she looks at me with joy in her eyes. "We won't have much time, children," she says, waving us to the table and shooting a meaningful look at Cassian. "For safety's sake."

"I've taken all the steps—"

"There are other events. You heard of the king."

The king. The king Lysander mentioned.

"And the son," she says, dropping her voice. "Exile."

"Surely that won't touch us here." Cassian sounds confident, but I'm not so sure.

"We must watch the pieces on the board." She reaches out and pats his hand. "But right now, we need to eat.

And you must tell me everything. Start from the beginning. How did you find her?"

Cassian looks at me across the table and takes my hand in his. "Life brought her to me against her will," he says, his voice thick with meaning. "But then I couldn't let her go."

AUTHOR'S NOTE

Dearest readers,

Hello, and welcome to 2019! This is my first published work of the year, and the hardest one of my career so far to write. And while it's written with all the Wilde love and style you've come to expect, I know the subject matter is a different from what's come before.

In a way, this is because the latter half of 2018 was not particularly kind to me in my personal life. Or my writing life, for that matter. This book was meant to be finished many weeks ago, but it was not. In fact, for several months, I didn't write at all.

At times I thought maybe I wouldn't write again. I'd stare at the ceiling at night and consider the possibility that I should pack up my iPad and head for more temperate climes. Figuratively speaking, I mean, because I can't actually move cities or states at the moment.

In the end, I remembered why I started all this in the first place: because I love to write. I've always loved to write. I loved to write even when I did not know the basic rules of writing and started each word with a capital letter instead of each paragraph. (That was kindergarten. I had a lot to learn.)

When I finally did write again, the book was...well, kind of dark. And actually it was quite a bit darker than I originally envisioned. They never even get to go out to dinner! It was, however, the one story that wouldn't rest until it was finished.

But it wasn't a solo adventure, getting to the end of this book. Not by far. So I wanted to take a moment and thank the people who stuck with me when I was at my lowest.

THANK YOU.

To my author friends, a lot of whom have been with me since 2016 and entertained a lot of half-baked ideas while I tried to figure out what to do. I'm afraid to make a list here because I'll forget someone and it'll be devastating, but you guys are a lot more to me than names who pop up in chat or on my phone. I really didn't want to let you down and you never gave up on me. Without you, I'd have taken my bindle and headed for the non-writing hills. Special thanks for answering my messages even when I'm sure it was a drag and listening to me call you and cry about dumb stuff like ads. It's fine—just write the books.

To Willow Winters, for having the idea for Cards of Love

in the first place and letting me be part of it. Being a member of such an awesome group is at least 50% of what kept me going, or at least made me start writing again. You couldn't *pay* me to stay away (sorry)!

To my editors, especially Kayla and Sara, who keep taking last-minute editing requests from me because I've spent too much time wallowing and left my writing until the very end, and who keep telling me they need my words in their lives.

To Skye Warren, who gave me more advice and encouragement than I ever could have hoped for, and who organized Romance Author Mastermind 2018, which changed my life.

To Becca Mysoor, who called me on the phone and made plans for me to get my work done and still kept calling even after I blew off all those plans to sulk and watch Netflix.

To every single one of the authors who agreed to come to my release party and celebrate this book. Your kindness showed me that there is still a place for me here.

To Kristin, who has answered between thirty and sixty texts that read *what if I can't do this???* with grace and compassion and replies that read *you can and you will.*

To all my readers, who welcomed me back with open arms even after I disappeared for weeks on end. I write because of you.

To Anna, who finished this book first of all my Wilde-

Cats, and to the rest of the WildeCats. You waited for me a long time. I can't express my gratitude for your patience and your sharp eyes. And to my advance reader Queens and the Wilde Women of Let's Get Wilde, your enthusiasm brightens my days. I hope you know how much.

To Amanda, who *literally* started the WildeCats for me when I couldn't do anything. I'd probably still be doing nothing without you.

To my sister, who suggested that perhaps extreme stress and creativity aren't buddies and that writer's block was not, in fact, an individual failing of mine. I can't imagine you'll ever read this, but you bailed me out when nobody else would and gave our girls some truly magical memories. I owe you, forever.

To my husband Josh, who listened to me sob about how I was ruining our lives, told me that I wasn't, and brought me everything I wanted to eat on a moment's notice. I've loved you since before you were hot, though I honestly can't remember what middle school was like. You're my second-chance hero and the reason I know that love can and does conquer all. Rumi says that *out beyond ideas of rightdoing and wrongdoing there is a field.* I'll meet you there.

To my girls, who think that the only reason I could be crying is that I might miss my parents. Missing their parents is the worst thing they can imagine. For them, writing is only a small part of me. If I never wrote another word again, they would still think I was amazing. I love them like that, too.

Finally, to Justice, who knows the wretched feeling of having royally screwed up and the complicated pleasure of finally facing the consequences, even if the two aren't meant to be connected. And to Cassian, who knows how heavy the world is on a person's shoulders and how light it can be when you remember that friends and loved ones are all that matter when everything is said and done.

If I forgot you in this list, I'm sorry, and thank you too. My heart is overflowing, seriously. It's making me cry, a little bit, and the thing is...I have to go ahead and publish this book.

So here's to a truly kickass 2019 and to pushing boundaries whenever they cry out to be pushed (or, like, spanked—oh, god, I'll see myself out). This community is the best and I wouldn't trade it for the world. I wouldn't even trade it for Netflix, though for a while I really tried. Thank you, endlessly, for having me.

<3 Amelia

P.S. If you've read this far, you deserve a special reward, so here it is. Cassian and Justice have had their HEA, but there is more afoot in their world in a tiny country across the ocean. Read all about it in Broken Crown by yours truly, out in 2019.

DRAW YOUR NEXT CARD

JUSTICE is just one of the many stories in the Cards of Love Collection. Which card will you choose next?

https://cardsofloveromance.com

For more books by Amelia Wilde, visit her online at
www.awilderomance.com